Magical Wonder Tales

MAGICAL
WONDER TALES

KING BEETLE TAMER AND OTHER STORIES

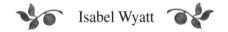 Isabel Wyatt

Floris Books

First published in 1980
This third edition published in 2013 by Floris Books

Previous edition published as *King Beetle-Tamer*
And Other Light-Hearted Wonder Tales

British Library CIP Data available
ISBN 978-178250-009-4
Printed in Great Britain
by Bell & Bain Ltd, Glasgow

Contents

1. King Beetle Tamer   7
2. Ogo and the Sun Horse   22
3. Roll Away the Stone   34
4. The Root of Healing   44
5. The Prince Who Lost His Shadow   50
6. The Unicorn's Fosterling   58
7. The Gorgeous Nightingale   67
8. The King's Candle   74
9. Rose and Lily   84
10. The Terrible Tanterabogus   95
11. Cocorico and Coquelicot   109
12. The Mirror on the Mountain   118
13. The Four-Leaved Clover   131
14. The Shining Loaf   139
15. King Arthur's Gold   146

1. King Beetle Tamer

Orfeo was born on the same day that his father died.

One evening, one year later, when Orfeo was asleep in an oak cradle in his mother's kitchen, an old travelling woman knocked at the door of the tumbledown cottage. She asked Orfeo's mother for a bit of bread to eat.

"Come in and rest by the fire while you eat," invited Orfeo's mother.

While the old woman rested by the fire, she peered into the cradle at the sleeping child.

"Och, he's a broth of a boy!" she wheezed, which is something people said in Ireland to mean that he looked like a good, strong baby.

"Indeed, he is," agreed his mother, just like any mother would.

"He'll grow into a happy young man," said the old woman.

"Indeed, he will," said his mother.

"He will die in his bed," said the old woman.

"Indeed we do, around here," said his mother.

"But you don't die young, or from being crushed by a

falling wall," said the old woman, "as this young boy might do. But, if he's lucky, he will be king after the king."

The summer that Orfeo became a happy young man (as tall and skinny as two yards of pump water), his mother made him leave his box bed by the kitchen chimney wall, and sent him to sleep outdoors, as far away from walls as he could get.

"I'm doing this for your sake, love of my life, my treasure," she told him. "What kind of mother would I be if I let a falling wall stop you from being king?"

Orfeo didn't complain, and went to sleep in the meadow. But each time he lay down in the grass, he was worried about hurting lots of insects and creeping things. So he would stamp three times to warn them, and give them time to get safely away. And away they all flew and scuttled and scurried for dear life.

But as soon as Orfeo had settled down, looking up at the evening star in the sunset sky, back they all came.

"He is as sweet as a long streak of honey," cried the ladybirds, each standing on her six legs to admire him. "And, look, his nose has ladybird freckles all over it!"

"What is more, he is kind," said their menfolk, each waving his two front legs to mark his words. "From now on, he is our friend and king."

The creeping things told the field mice, and the field mice told the birds. When Orfeo woke at dawn, he had a welcome fit for a French king, with the songbirds making chamber music, the butterflies fluttering about him, and all the little meadow creatures standing round and bowing like real courtiers.

And all that summer, Orfeo slept out in the meadow.

When autumn came, Orfeo's mother died. And as the nights grew longer and colder, Orfeo thought, "While she was alive, I slept outdoors so she wouldn't worry. But in her heart she knew that you must face danger, not run away from it. What will happen will happen, wherever I sleep."

So he came indoors and slept in the box bed in the kitchen again, snug and cosy against the warm chimney wall.

Soon the night frosts came: nine white ones in a row, and then a black one which left the meadow burned up with its freezing fire. When Orfeo went outside on the tenth morning, he heard little voices coming from the ruined grass. "Orfeo, Orfeo, you are our friend and king. We can't stay in this frosty grass. Please can we spend the winter in the walls of your cottage?"

"With all my heart, yes!" cried Orfeo. He held the kitchen door wide open and all the little creatures flew, scuttled and scurried inside. Beetles' wing cases shut with a click, and shrews' tails vanished like bits of string, as they tucked themselves away in each nook and cranny.

In fact, they tucked themselves away so well that at first Orfeo hardly knew they were there. But as they grew more at home, they woke up now and then and crept out of their beds to keep him company. The crickets would sing on the hearth in the dusk when Orfeo sat by the fire. On days of winter sun, butterflies hanging with folded wings in dark corners would flutter to his finger tip, to bask in the warmth. The mice would creep out from their holes in the skirting board and sit up to beg for crumbs, their whiskers twitching, their eyes as bright as beads.

One day, Orfeo's neighbours came to him and said, "Orfeo, you must get your cottage in order. Winter is the best time to do repairs, when you're not busy with other things. Tell us when you're ready, and we'll give you a hand."

Orfeo thanked them and said, "Let's put it off until spring. I have winter guests and it would be a pity to disturb them."

The winter wore on but then on February first, St Bridget's Day, with the first smell of spring on the way, Orfeo's winter guests woke wide awake and streamed outdoors again.

"*Now* I can put my cottage in order," said Orfeo.

But already the birds had begun to put on their courting colours, and to choose their sweethearts; and only a fortnight later came St Valentine's Day, when the birds get married. Pair by pair they came to Orfeo, and bowed to him with their wing tips on their hearts, and told him he was their friend and king. They asked if they could please build their nests on the outside of his cottage – the starlings in the thatch, the jackdaws in the chimney, the swallows under the eaves, the bluetits in the ivy, and the robins in the crumbling niches in the wall.

"With all my heart, yes!" cried Orfeo.

What a coming and going there was then, with beakfuls of sticks and straw and hay and mud and horsehair and everything else good for home-making. And when the nests were finished and full of eggs, each mother bird kept them warm with the living quilt of her own body, and a choir of proud fathers sang around Orfeo's tumbledown cottage!

Orfeo's neighbours came to him again, and said, "Orfeo, that chimney wall will fall down around your ears if you do not mend it, and soon we shall be too busy to help you."

Orfeo thanked them and said, "Let's put it off until summer. I have spring guests and it would be a pity to disturb them." He didn't want to disturb the jackdaw, even though its nest make his chimney smoke badly.

The spring wore on. The eggs hatched and from dawn to dusk, the parent birds flew to and fro, to and fro, filling the gaping mouths of their little nestlings. Then the baby birds grew feathers and still the parent birds flew to and fro, to and fro, teaching their fledglings to fly.

"As soon as the baby birds can fly," said Orfeo, "*then* I can put my cottage in order."

But before the baby birds could fly, the hive bees began to swarm. Now in those days only straw hives were used; the box hives of today, in which the bees can live year after year, had not yet been invented. When people took honey from straw hives once a year, they had to stifle the bees with sulphur smoke. And so this year one wise old queen bee made up her mind to save them from this fate.

Leaving the parent hive one warm May morning, with her worker bees streaming behind her, she made a beeline to

Orfeo and settled on his nose. The first worker bees clung to her, and more worker bees streamed behind her, till a ball of bees, like a rich, brown, seething plum pudding, was hanging from the end of Orfeo's nose.

"Orfeo, Orfeo, you are our friend and king," piped the queen bee from the middle of this mass. "Please can we make our new home in your rafters?"

"With all my heart, yes!" cried Orfeo.

So the bees streamed into Orfeo's kitchen, and at once were as busy as bees can be in the rafters. Soon there were white, gleaming combs of six-sided cells hanging from the thick black beams, and in some of the cells the queen was laying eggs for all she was worth, while in others golden honey and bee-bread were being stored as fast as the nectar and pollen they were made from were brought in from the flowers.

"Now I *can't* set my cottage in order," said Orfeo to himself, "for these guests will be with me the whole year through."

Winter came round again. The insects came indoors to shelter in nooks and crannies; the field mice came back to their mouse holes; the crickets sang again on the hearth. Those birds who had not flocked south for the winter came back to their old family homes in thatch and wall and ivy, and the sparrows moved into the swallows' empty houses under the eaves. The bees' humming among the rafters had stopped; the workers clung to the queen in a sleeping ball.

The winter storms set in. The winter winds roared and howled round the chimney. But Orfeo slept snug and sound in his warm bed; and all his two-legged, four-legged and six-legged guests slept snug and sound in theirs.

One night, the quiet kitchen was lit dimly by a stable lantern hung beside the door. Suddenly, the whole kitchen was invaded by every insect and creeping thing that had been tucked up in the nooks and crannies of the chimney wall, while out of its mouse holes scuttled generations of mice, from bald old great-grandfathers to bright-eyed babes.

They swarmed over the sleeping Orfeo. They tickled his face, the insects with their feet, the mice with their whiskers; and as soon as they felt his eyelids flutter, they chanted all together, "Orfeo, Orfeo, you are our friend and king. Please let us tell you that the wind has broken the chimney wall, and it is about to fall!"

In one bound, Orfeo was out of his bed. In a wave of mice and insects, a blast of wind blew him to the other side of the room. There was a crash and a roar; the air was thick with dust. As it cleared, Orfeo saw a huge, jagged gap in the chimney wall; and below it, under a heap of stones and rubble, his box bed was smashed to smithereens.

The chimney jackdaw came flying through the hole in the wall. He began to beat with his wings at the fallen stones, to scrabble at them with beak and claws, all the time squawking, "My ring! My ruby! My ring!"

Orfeo lifted the stable lantern from its hook and, holding it close, lifted stone after stone from the crushed bed to the floor, until he came to the jackdaw's nest, squashed as flat as a pancake. In it something glowed red like an ember.

Orfeo picked it up and held it close to the lantern. It was a large ruby, set in a small golden ring. The ruby was cut like a half-open rose, and round it, in letters of gold, ran the name *Roselle*.

"It is mine, Orfeo! It is mine!" squawked the jackdaw, taking flying, pecking leaps at it.

"Since when did jackdaws wear rings?" asked Orfeo. "And since when is your name Roselle?"

"Roselle is a princess," the jackdaw told him. "She put the ring down by her open window while she washed her hands. And the next thing I knew, I was flying home with it in my beak."

"This ring belongs to the princess, jackdaw, not to you," said Orfeo. "You must give it back."

"I could pop it on her window ledge when no one is looking," suggested the jackdaw hopefully.

"No," said Orfeo firmly, "because then someone innocent might be blamed. You must give it back into her own hands."

"They will wring my neck," wailed the jackdaw. "Orfeo, Orfeo, you are my friend and king. Please will *you* give it back for me – they will not wring your neck."

Orfeo thought for a moment, and then agreed to take the ring to the princess.

Orfeo set out at dawn, leaving his tumbledown cottage just as it was with the huge hole in its wall. At noon he reached the gates of the king's town and wondered, as he made his way towards the king's palace, why he didn't meet a soul.

But in the square in front of the palace he found men standing as close as ears of corn in a cornfield. Every upper window was crowded, and there was not a face in all that sea of faces that was not turned towards the palace.

Orfeo was so tall that, standing on his toes and craning his long neck, he could see right over all those heads. What he saw was a long line of riders, all as colourful as parrots, coming through the palace gates between two rows of footmen wearing black and white, bowing like penguins.

"Who are they?" Orfeo asked a man at a window overhead.

"That's today's batch of princes returning the princess's ring," the man chuckled.

"Has she lost that many?" Orfeo marvelled.

"Only one," the man told him, still chuckling. "But the finder will marry her and be king after the king; so everywhere rings are being found to left and right."

Flattening himself against the fronts of the houses, Orfeo edged his way towards the palace gates. When the last of the parrot princes had ridden in, he, too, stepped forward.

At the sight of his tall, skinny beanpole of a figure, dressed in a peasant's smock and topped by a thatch of hair as rough as a rook's nest, a great bellow of good-natured laughter shook the crowd. The footmen lifted haughty noses and would have clashed the gates in his face; but when he opened his palm and showed them what was hidden there, their eyes jumped out of their heads, and they let him in.

In the grand royal chamber, Orfeo saw the king sitting hawk-eyed on his throne, while on a lower throne beside him sat a bright-haired princess, as small and charming as a golden-crested wren.

Each prince came in turn before the king, bowed and explained how he had found his ring, and then knelt to place it on the finger of the princess. Each time, she sat and stared at the ring, then shook her bright head sadly; each time, a murmur passed round the chamber: *"The ring did not light up!"*

At last only Orfeo was left. As he stepped forward to bow, people started to laugh behind his back; and as, in his kind, slow voice he told his story, the parrot princes rocked with laughter. The king sat grim and tight-lipped, staring hard at Orfeo.

But when Orfeo knelt and placed the ring on Princess Roselle's finger, it flamed into such a sunburst of splendour that every face in the chamber was washed by its crimson light; and this time the murmur grew to a roar: *"The right ring has been found!"*

The princess lifted her head, and looked at Orfeo; and the smile she gave him went straight from her heart to his.

"Father," she said, "this is my ring, and this is the man I shall marry."

At this, the king's hair stood on end with rage, so that his crown flew up into the air, then fell back on his head with a plop. "What, marry a peasant?" he exploded. "Have you taken leave of your senses? Go now to the Rose Tower till you find them again! As for you, my fine beetle tamer, you can thank your stars I am letting you off with merely kicking you out of my palace!"

Rough hands seized Orfeo and dragged him out of the

royal chamber, and hearty kicks sped him out of the palace. Orfeo wandered around alleys for a while, then went back to the town gates. He sat down to think, in the shelter of the buttress that held up the town wall.

Soon people came running to the town gates, to see the princess pass by on her way to the Rose Tower.

"Mother, what *is* a Rose Tower?" Orfeo heard a child's shrill voice ask.

"It is where the king shuts people up till they do what he tells them," the mother answered.

"I would run away if he put *me* there," said the child.

"No one yet has ever escaped the Rose Tower," his mother told him. "It is right on the edge of a cliff, and it has three high walls all round it. Look – look! Here she comes!"

Murmurs of pity and love rose from the crowd as the princess's carriage went past, with guards on either side.

"But there are two princesses in it, Mother," piped the child, "both with golden hair."

"The one this side is the princess," his mother told him. "The other is Lady Rosina, her cousin and lady-in-waiting."

Behind the carriage rumbled a wagon, laden with food and clothing. Last of all walked two of the palace porters, carrying a big wicker basket between them by its ear-shaped handles.

"What's that basket for, Mother?" the child piped up again.

"For the roses," his mother told him. "Red roses bloom around the Rose Tower all the year round. When the princess fills that basket with roses and sends it to the king, it will tell him she has given in, and then he will let her out."

"I wish *I* had that basket. It would be lovely to hide in," said the child.

Hidden behind the buttress, Orfeo could have jumped for joy. The child's chatter had shown him just how to rescue the princess.

When the crowd had drifted home, Orfeo rose and followed the wagon's wheel tracks out of the town and through the forest to the cliff top. He saw how the tower and its rose garden were hemmed in by its three high walls. He could quite see why no one yet had ever escaped.

"No one until now," he said to himself. "But no one has had the help of a beetle tamer and his winter guests."

He tramped back to his tumbledown cottage and held a meeting with his guests. A clapping of wings, paws and front legs greeted the plan he put before them.

"Orfeo, Orfeo, you are our friend and king," they all chanted. "For you we would do far, far more than this."

First, Orfeo sent the jackdaw to Rose Tower. He landed on the window ledge at the top of the tower and thrust his black head through the open casement. When he saw Roselle and Rosina, he squawked, "Princess, Orfeo is coming to rescue you with thousands and thousands of friends. But he needs your help."

Roselle and Rosina ran to the window. Their faces grew bright with hope, and they nodded their golden heads, as the jackdaw told them the whole plan.

When the jackdaw had flown away, Rosina helped the princess into her royal robes of purple velvet. She set her golden crown on her golden head, and her ruby ring on her finger. Then Rosina hid in her bedchamber.

The princess rang a silver bell. She was alone when two guards answered it. "I am ready to send the king my father his basket of roses," she said. "Bring them up here for me to arrange."

She was still alone when they brought the basket, heaped high with red roses. "Send the porters up in half an hour," she told them, "to take the basket to the palace."

As soon as the guards had gone, Rosina ran in from the bedchamber. Barring the door, they tipped out the roses and swiftly changed clothes. Wrapped in a rose-coloured cloak, the princess curled up in the bottom of the basket, and Rosina heaped the roses over her. She hid those that were left inside an old oak chest.

When, half an hour later, the porters knocked at the door, Rosina was standing before the window, her back to the light, dressed in Roselle's royal robes of purple velvet, with Roselle's golden crown on her own golden head. The great ruby flashed on her finger as she motioned them to take the basket. If asked, they would have sworn it was the princess herself they had seen.

The porters lifted up the basket of roses, and carried it down spiral after spiral of the corkscrew stairs. The guards unlocked the heavy door of the tower and the gates of the three high walls for them; and out they passed into the forest, the basket of heaped roses swinging between them.

They walked in silence for a while. Then one of them said, "It did not take the princess long to give in. A pity. I liked the look of that beetle tamer."

"I did too," said the other. "He had the makings of a good king."

They walked in silence for a while further. Then the first said, "Roses weigh more than you would think."

"There's a lot of iron in roses," said the second.

They walked in silence for a little longer. Then the first, glancing up, gave a loud yelp of terror; and the second, glancing down, gave an even louder cry.

For all around them, as far as the eye could see, the air was thick with birds and beetles, in their thousands and their thousands of thousands, all flying towards them as fast as their wings could carry them.

And all around them, as far as the eye could see, the ground was covered with every kind of small, four-footed creature, in their thousands and their thousands of thousands, all racing towards them with teeth bared and the most bloodthirsty look on their furry faces.

"Run for your life!" cried both porters together. And they dropped the basket of roses and ran as if all the monsters in the world were chasing them, as indeed they thought they were.

Then out from among the trees rode Orfeo on a shaggy wild pony, leading its twin by a halter of heather rope. Roselle heard him and jumped out of the basket, scattering a blanket of red roses on the grass. He helped her onto her pony and away they galloped to his tumbledown cottage, Roselle's rose-coloured cloak flying behind her. Then Orfeo sent the jackdaw at once to tell the king their news.

"Well, well! There is more in this beetle tamer," cried the king, "than in all those parrot princes!" And he laughed at how Orfeo and Roselle had outwitted him, laughing so much that his crown slipped to one side. Then he sent the jackdaw back to tell Roselle and her beetle tamer to come home to the palace at once and have a fine wedding.

This they did, and Rosina was the chief bridesmaid. And when, after a time, the king died, Orfeo became king after all. He was a king of everyone's heart, and throughout the land and all his long life, his people called him King Beetle Tamer.

2. Ogo and the Sun Horse

Malvaizia was a wicked old witch. She was as wrinkled as a walnut, and as grey as the grey mist; her cold eyes were as unblinking as a lizard's; for hair she had clumps of drab seaweed; and her teeth gnashed like the whirr and grind of millstones.

She lived in a cave on the seashore with Ogo, her cheeky rascal of a son who like stealing things. When she sat with one foot on the sand and the other in the sea, she could put spells on both land and water.

She wore a pet octopus draped like a cloak around her craggy shoulders, its head behind her own like a hood. Stuck in her belt of sea-serpent skin were the three sharpest things in the world: a needle made out of a crab's claw, a spindle made out of shark's teeth and a swordfish's sword.

"Read me my fortune," Ogo said to his mother one day.

Malvaizia took her needle from her belt and prodded the octopus with it. "Squirt!" she barked.

The octopus squirted. It squirted a jet of sepia ink into a rock basin at the mouth of the cave. The old witch bent over the inky pool and stared, without a wink or a blink of her cold lizard eyes, into its murky depths.

"Ogo!" she chortled. "Do you know that you will be the very first man to go all the way around the world in twenty-three hours?"

"Shall I, indeed?" snorted Ogo. "And how and when shall I die?"

Again the old witch bent and stared, without a wink or a blink of her cold lizard eyes, into the murky depths of the inky pool.

"You are supposed to die in a sword test," she reported. "But you can avoid that if you kidnap a small wind."

"Pah! Nothing easier," boasted Ogo. And away he went, bounding and bouncing, till he came to Windy Corner. This was where the winds who cleaned the air lived. The small winds, their babies, were tucked up cosily in leafy cradles, swinging from the branches of Windy Corner's bushes. They rocked and slept peacefully while their mothers were out at work, sweeping the clouds from the sky and the fallen leaves from the fields.

Now Ogo lived by stealing; you could say he even lived *for* stealing. He was the most light-fingered boy in the whole world. So to him it was nothing, nothing at all, to snatch a small wind from its cradle. He kidnapped one so skilfully and smoothly that he had it out and away and home in his cave, and it did not even wake up.

Malvaizia took it from him, popped it into a bladder of some bladderwrack, and hung the tiny sack among her seaweed hair.

"Hide one among many," she cackled, "and who will see it there?"

Just then a frantic mother wind swept by with streaming hair and streaming eyes. She had just gone home to Windy Corner and found her cradle empty. Her eyes passed, unseeing, over her small wind's prison; and on she went, moaning, to and fro, to and fro around the world, seeking her child, pouncing on each small sound in the frantic hope it might be her lost darling.

"Who will see it there indeed?" smirked Ogo.

Ogo was such a master thief that his cave was chock-a-block with stolen treasure of every size and shape and colour and sort and kind. As he was roaming and rootling among them later that day, he suddenly yawned and said, "I have stolen every single thing worth stealing within a day's march of my cave. Look in your inky pool, mother, and find me somewhere new to loot."

"Find it yourself," snapped Malvaizia. "Why don't you steal a horse from the sun? It will carry you right around the earth in twenty-three hours, and there won't be a thing worth stealing in the whole world that you won't see."

"I'll do that, so I will!" cried Ogo briskly.

A quickbeam tree grew on the cliff above the cave. Malvaizia climbed up the cliff, clinging with tooth and nail, and cut a thin branch from it with her swordfish sword.

"Nothing makes an enchanted horse behave like a quickbeam riding crop," she told Ogo as she handed it over. "Here, you had better take my fish sword, too. Nothing else will be sharp enough to cut that horse's straps."

Ogo took them both and away he went, bounding and bouncing towards the east, for he knew that the sun's chariot only paused awile at Sunrise Point. On he went, bounding and bouncing, bouncing and bounding, till he came to a rose bush bearing two golden roses and beside it a wheat stalk bearing two golden ears of wheat. A stream of clear water flowed nearby. And so he knew he had come to Sunrise Point.

He wriggled himself right under a rock, like an insect. Night fell. All night long he lay there and, one by one, felt the three colds of night creep upon him. First it grew as cold as a coffin, and he knew from this that it was midnight. Then it grew as cold as a wind blowing under a sail, and he knew from this that it was three o'clock, when the earth's breathing changes. Then it grew as cold as Malvaizia's eyes, and he knew from this that dawn was near.

Then Ogo saw the sun's golden chariot approaching. He heard the sun calling out to the two sun horses, who pulled the chariot, to pause and rest awhile. So the horses stopped by the stream of clear water, stooped their golden necks, and drank. The sun stepped down from his golden chariot and groomed each horse in turn. He plucked the two golden roses and braided them into their manes; he plucked the two golden wheat ears and braided them into their tails. At once, two new roses began to bud on the rose bush, and on the wheat stalk two wheat ears began to swell, ready for dawn the next day.

When the sun went around to the far side of his horses, Ogo wriggled out from beneath his stone and crept nearer, his body rippling along the ground like a snake's. One slash with Malvaizia's fish sword, and he had cut the nearest horse free of his straps; one leap, and he sat astride him; one flick of the quickbeam riding crop, and *whish-whoosh* went the golden wings of the golden sun horse as he sprang and soared into flight.

No wind in the whole world could equal the speed of that sun horse. So swiftly and so strongly did the horse fly that Ogo felt like no more than a wisp of straw on his back. His knees gripped the horse's flanks as close as bark grips its tree, and away he went, away, away, around the wonderful racecourse of the sky.

And away around the course of the sky behind him, the sun drove, frantic and furious. But the sun's golden chariot was too heavy for only one horse; it tilted and tipped and rocked and rolled and staggered; further and further and ever further it fell behind.

Everywhere on the earth below, men and women cried out at the sight of the golden sun horse and his rider sweeping *whish-whoosh* overhead, and at the sight of the sun in his chariot struggling painfully behind. And everywhere on the earth below, Ogo saw such treasures crying out to be stolen that his fingers itched to lift them then and there.

But the most priceless treasure of them all was the one he had already stolen. He knew that he could never bear to let this golden sun horse out of his hands again. "In any case," he mused, "I shall need him for when I go robbing and raiding around the world."

So, as he came up from the other side of the earth to Sunrise Point an hour before sunrise was due (for he had galloped around the earth in only twenty-three hours), he turned his horse's head towards Malvaizia's cave.

As he flew over the quickbeam tree on the cliff above the cave, he gave the sun horse a vicious cut with the quickbeam riding crop, bringing him down to earth with such a jar that a petal flew out from the golden rose braided into his mane, and a golden wheat ear came loose from his tail. Sparks flew from his golden hoofs as he galloped over the rocks, before the cave swallowed his brightness.

Back at Sunrise Point, the sun's young servant, Sunface, his face as bright as the golden goblet in his hands, had come in the night. He brought wine to comfort the sad heart of his lord. As he stood waiting, he felt, one by one, the first two colds of night creep upon him.

First it grew as cold as a coffin, and he knew from this that it was midnight. Then it grew as cold as a wind blowing under a sail, and he knew from this that it was three o'clock, when the earth's breathing changes.

But before the third cold crept upon him, the sky grew red with a false and fleeting sunrise, as Ogo on his sun horse came galloping up from the other side of the earth. He came in a flash; he went in a flash; he came and went too swiftly to notice the bright face and the bright cup of wine gleaming softly between the rose bush and the stalk of wheat. He came and went too swiftly for Sunface to stop him in mid-flight, but Sunface's eye followed the flash and marked the way he went.

27

After a while it grew as cold as Malvaizia's eyes, and Sunface knew from this that the time for the true dawn was at hand. Yet still the true dawn tarried a while longer, till at last the sun came struggling up into the sky with one weary sun horse. It had taken him twenty-five hours to drive around the earth.

When the sun had gratefully drunk the wine from the golden goblet, Sunface begged him, "Lord, please let me follow the horse thief and bring your sun horse home."

"Stretch your right palm out," replied the sun. "I will give you a gift for the road."

Sunface stretched out his right palm. The sun touched it with the light that streamed from his own finger tips. "On the earth it is hard to tell truth from lies," he said. "But if any earth-being lies to you now, your right palm will shoot out fire."

The sun horse harnessed to the chariot drank from the clear stream, but sadly, because he was missing his friend. Sunface groomed him; he plucked one of the golden roses and braided it into his mane; he plucked one of the golden wheat ears and braided it into his tail. And at once a second rose began to bud, and a second wheat ear began to swell.

Then the sun took up his golden reins and drove his chariot on to bring day to the world; and Sunface, as light and as bright and as quick and as neat as a sunbeam, went speeding in the direction in which he had seen Ogo and the stolen sun horse go.

A lingering line of faint and fading brightness in the air led him as far as the quickbeam tree on the cliff above the cave, but here the brightness ended as abruptly as if cut off with a knife. As he stood beneath the tree, searching around him, he saw that one of its branches had been severed, and he drew his sword to heal the wound with its sunbeam blade. At the rattle of the scabbard, the mother wind, in sudden hope, came sweeping up from the seashore.

She sighed when her eyes fell on Sunface. "It is you, Sunface, not my little lost child. If you are seeking the stolen sun horse, I heard the *whish-whoosh* of his wings just here in the night, and the clang of his hoofs on the rocks by the witch's cave. It is strange how my heart keeps drawing me back to that cave. Come with me; I will show you."

Sunface followed her down the cliff, his bright face flashing a streak of light on the air, so that Ogo, peering from the cave, exclaimed, "Look, Mother! A star is falling to earth!"

"Better if it were," cried Malvaizia as she joined him. "That is the face of the sun's servant, hot on the tracks of his horse. Quick, let me get out and put one foot on sand and one in the sea, to spin a spell to save your new treasure!"

When Sunface followed the mother wind down to the seashore, he found a grey old woman sitting on a rock, with one bare foot on the sand and the other in the sea, her seaweed hair covering her from top to toe, and a captive octopus draped like a cloak around her craggy shoulders, its head behind her own like a hood. There she sat, spinning a seaweed cord on her sharp shark-tooth spindle, muttering away to herself, grinning and grimacing and gnashing her huge teeth with a whirr and grind of millstones.

"Good morning to you!" Sunface greeted her gravely. She

gave no greeting back, but went on with her dark muttering. All she gave him was a look, and that look was as ugly as a bad deed.

But the mother wind's ears, sharpened with grief, caught a fainter sound from the base of Malvaizia's rock. She blew down to it in sudden hope that it might be her child, blowing aside the witch's concealing strands of seaweed hair and blowing the golden rose petal up into Sunface's hand. The witch had been scraping it into the sand with her bare heel.

Not a wink, not a blink, did those lizard eyes give; nor did the witch for an instant cease muttering and spluttering, grinning and grinding, spinning and spell binding.

But again the mother wind's grief-sharpened ears caught a delicate sound – a slight dry rustle amid the damp slap and flap of the seaweed turning, the twisting, coiling and cording, on the shark-tooth spindle. Up to it she blew with renewed hope, taking the seaweed cord in her teeth and shaking it till it snapped; and out of it fell, right at the feet of Sunface, a golden ear of wheat.

Still not a wink, not a blink, did those lizard eyes give. But the muttering and the spluttering ceased, and the grinning and the grinding ceased; for the seaweed cord had snapped, and with it the spell the old witch had been spinning.

At last Sunface spoke again. "Lady, where is your son?"

They say that an ostrich can hatch her egg with a look. That was the sort of look the old witch gave Sunface then, – so piercing that it could have cracked an egg.

"My house is near, but my son is far," she snapped.

At once Sunface felt his right palm shoot out fire. "Not as far as he has been, I think," he said. "Has he not been all around the world lately?" And he began to walk towards the cave.

At this the old witch gave a warning cackle, which brought Ogo running at top speed out of the cave.

"What do you want?" he shouted angrily.

"A stolen sun horse," Sunface told him mildly.

"Horse?" blustered Ogo. "There are no horses here."

For a second time, Sunface felt his right palm shoot out fire. "Surely I can hear one stamping," he said, as a clatter came from the cave.

"That is my grindstone," Ogo barked back.

For a third time, Sunface felt his right palm shoot out fire. "Surely I can hear one whinnying," he said, and this time it was so plain that even Ogo could not deny it.

"That is a seahorse out in the bay," he blustered again.

For a fourth time, Sunface felt his right palm shoot out fire. "Let's put this to the sword test," he challenged. "We will both fling up our swords. The sword of the one who speaks truth will fall *before* him; the sword of the one who lies will fall *on* him."

Malvaizia nodded vigorously, looking as smug as a cat who has licked the cream-pot clean. All that had been obscure in the inky pool was now clear to her. Under her seaweed hair her right hand grasped her needle, and her left hand held the bladder in which the small wind was hidden.

Sunface flung up his sun sword. It left an arc in the

air that shimmered like a rainbow. It fell with the point downward and stood upright and quivering in the sand before his feet.

Ogo flung up his fish sword. Malvaizia pricked the bladder, and, with a whimper, out rushed the little wind. *Puff* went the little wind; it was just the right strength, as Malvaizia knew it would be, to blow Ogo's sword a step forward into safety as it fell.

But the mother wind had heard her lost baby's cry. She blew headlong to embrace it; and the rush of her coming blew the sword briskly back. It fell, point downward, on Ogo, and Ogo fell lifeless onto the sand.

At this, Malvaizia rose up, shrieking, and the octopus hanging from her craggy shoulders began to stir its arms. A mighty wave swept in and over the rock, and when it was sucked noisily back, Ogo and Malvaizia were there no longer, and something that looked like a giant starfish was floating out to sea.

While the mother wind blew happily home to Windy Corner, her baby in her arms, Sunface went into the cave. He led the golden sun horse out and leaped onto its back. *Whish-whoosh* went the golden wings; a streak of light flashed upward through the air and Sunface didn't need a quickbeam riding crop to urge on the eager horse.

At dawn when the sun came up from the other side of the earth at Sunrise Point, there was much rejoicing. The two sun horses drank together happily from the stream; happily Sunface groomed them, braiding a fresh rose into each mane, a fresh wheat ear into each tail; happily he watched the sun set out on his radiant journey. Everywhere, grateful and celebrating, trees lifted up their arms, and men and women their faces, and blessed the sun and his servant who had made the world right again. And once more the golden chariot drove around the earth in twenty-four hours, and has done so ever since.

3. Roll Away the Stone

Marigold was a small child, bare from top to toe, who fell, one day, into the forest. She fell with a bump; all in an instant, where she was, there she was.

It was dark, and all around her was gloom as grey as ashes, between trees as black as soot. And it was lonely; there was no one else in the forest except her.

Then, far off among the trees, she saw a spark of light. She ran towards it as fast as her bare little legs could carry her.

The spark grew into a little house, all glinting and glowing. Peeping in at a low window, Marigold saw a fire burning merrily on the hearth, as if it was very glad to be alive. In front of it a white doe, a female deer, lay stretched out contentedly. There were red candles burning brightly on a table, with supper laid around them on a linen cloth so white that it shone.

In the firelight and the candlelight sat a lady, working at a purring spinning wheel. Her face was so motherly that Marigold suddenly felt comforted.

As Marigold stood and stared in at the peaceful room, the

white doe lifted her head, ears pricked, towards the window; and at this the lady rose from her spinning and came to the door and opened it.

"Who is there?" she called softly into the night.

"Marigold," gulped Marigold.

"Come in by the warm fire, Marigold," said the lady kindly. She bent and helped her in. She sat her by the fire beside the white doe and tucked her up in a snug, soft shawl, before bringing her hot milk to drink.

Kneeling beside her, smiling, she touched a beauty spot between Marigold's eyebrows that was like a tiny marigold.

"Now I know why you are called Marigold," she said. "*My* name is Bona. Where do you come from, Marigold?"

Marigold thought hard. "I can *nearly* remember, but not quite," she said at last.

"*How* did you come, Marigold?" Bona asked her then.

"A big bird dropped me," Marigold told her promptly.

Marigold clutched a torn strip of fine linen in her left hand. Bona pulled it gently out and held it to the fire to examine it. It was exquisitely woven, in a design she had never seen before, with a gold thread fringing the material.

Staring through it at the fire, Bona saw a picture forming in the flames. She saw Marigold running up a flight of marble steps from a sunny lake in which she had been bathing; she saw her waving the towel in her hand at someone nearby; she saw a griffin swoop, attracted by the glitter of the golden fringe; she saw the tussle, and the towel tearing, and Marigold snatched up in a griffin's claws and carried high over the plains and forests – who could tell how far?

Marigold was lost and it would be impossible to find the way back to her home. But Bona lifted the lid of the big cedarwood chest in which she kept her woven cloths, and she laid the linen fragment carefully away with them.

Marigold stayed with Bona and became her foster child. Bona spun and wove garments for her, strong and brightly coloured. They fitted the carefree life she led, playing with the white doe, running happily in and out of the little forest house, helping Bona to keep it all glinting and glowing, gathering herbs in her garden and apples in her orchard.

"Do not stray too far into the forest, Marigold," Bona warned her one day, "in case you meet a tiger."

"Would a tiger not be friends with me?" asked Marigold in surprise. "The deer and the hares and the birds and the squirrels all are."

"We have wild beasts in the forests, too," Bona told her. "It is one of the king's hunting forests. Just in case you do ever meet one, we will cut you a hazel wand at the next full moon."

The orchard had a hedge of hazel bushes all round it, and at the full of the moon Bona and Marigold went along this with a silver knife. The bushes waved to and fro in the moonlight, and Bona looked each bush over till she found the most pliant branch of all – so pliant that, when she cut it, it twisted around itself like a rod entwined by two snakes.

"Carry it always in your belt," Bona said as she gave it to Marigold, "and if any wild beast threatens you, hold it firmly in your right hand and touch his heart with it."

"And what will *he* do then?" asked Marigold breathlessly.

"Oh, then," said Bona, "he will be your friend."

That night, as Bona and Marigold slept, an earthquake shook the forest. The little forest house fell in, so that its roof timbers lay lower than its floor timbers, its floor higher than its roof. When dawn came and Marigold crawled out from amid the wreckage, Bona and her white doe were nowhere to be seen.

Marigold searched for them near and far, calling their names with a breaking heart. As she wandered to and fro, she found that the very shape of the forest had changed. Fallen trees blocked the green paths she used to run along; the clear springs she used to drink from had been swallowed up. And at one place where there had been a landslide she came upon a cave that had been opened up.

"The little forest house is gone," thought Marigold. "I will make this cave my new home. At least it will give me shelter."

So she took whatever she could salvage from the ruins of the little house to this cave. She had to leave the big cedarwood chest, for it was broken; but she was glad to empty it of Bona's woven cloths to add a little warmth and cheer to her new bare home of rock. All she left behind was a rotting fragment of gold-fringed linen, which was caught on the splintered wood.

As she knelt in her new bare home of rock, coaxing a spark from flint and steel to light a fire, it suddenly got darker.

Whirling round, she saw that the lower part of the mouth of the cave was blocked and two green points were burning in the gloom.

"Who is there?" she called out bravely, though her voice *did* tremble a little.

The bulk blocking the entrance moved further into the cave; and as the light streamed in again Marigold saw a huge wild beast watching her with green eyes blazing and sharp teeth bared. His orange coat was striped with black.

"A *tiger* is here," he growled, deep in his throat. "And who are you?" And he made his whiskers fierce and bristled his tawny beard.

"Marigold," gulped Marigold, shaking with fright. But even in her fear she remembered Bona's warning, and her right hand flew to the hazel wand in her belt.

"Are you not afraid that I shall eat you, Marigold?" The tiger growled again, lashing his tail and unsheathing his cruel claws while his body crouched, ready to spring.

"Not w-while I have my hazel w-wand," stammered Marigold, holding it firmly and pointing it straight at his heart.

At this, all the wickedness ran out of the tiger, just like sawdust stuffing. He yawned a homely fireside yawn, stretched himself lazily and lay down, as relaxed and happy as a pet cat on a warm hearth rug.

Marigold leaned forward and touched the place where she thought a tiger would keep his heart with her hazel wand. His whiskers twitched and twinkled with pleasure, and he smiled most amiably.

"This is a fine cave," he purred. "Two could live here and be good company. Let's set up house in it together, and I will take care of you."

They set up house together in the cave, and Uncle Tiger, as Marigold liked to call him, became as fussy about Marigold's safety as an old hen with one chick. He prowled about the forest till he found a boulder just the right size for a fine front door, and between them they pushed and pulled it till in triumph they got it to the mouth of the cave.

"Each time I have to go out on tiger business, Marigold," he told her, "you must shut yourself indoors, and you must not open our fine front door till you hear me calling, *Marigold, Marigold, roll away the stone*! Now promise me, cross your heart."

And she crossed her heart and promised him.

Next day, while Uncle Tiger was out on tiger business, Marigold heard a loud uproar in the forest. She crouched, cowering, over the cave fire and blessed their fine front door, for it sounded as if all the wild beasts in the world were rampaging on the other side of it.

It was like music in her ears when at last she heard the tiger growl, "Marigold, Marigold, roll away the stone!"

She ran to obey and in staggered Uncle Tiger, puffing and panting and weary to the bone.

The very second he was inside, he closed their fine front door, then threw himself down by the fire and purred with pride like a kettle on the boil. "I led the king a fine dance today, when he came hunting in *my* forest! Did you hear his hounds yelping, and his horses thudding, and his hunters

39

shouting, and his horns going, *Tantivy, Tantivy*? If they were swift, I was swifter!"

"Oh, Uncle Tiger, *don't* go out tomorrow!" Marigold begged, alarmed. "You have saved yourself the first time, but you mightn't do so the second. What would I do if the king were to kill you?"

"Tush, first he would have to catch me," said the tiger. "But do not hang your bright little head and dim your beauty spot with worry. There will not be a second time, for the king never stays here more than one day. He will be hunting in some other tiger's forest tomorrow."

The king had indeed planned to do so. But as he and his hunters sat round their campfire that evening, eating before riding away, they started telling stories of the day's sport; and if the first story was far-fetched, those that followed were even more so, and the laughter grew louder with each one.

Presently one of the hunters said, "Now this is as true as that I sit here in this forest. I was hard on the tiger's heels when he reached his den. A rock blocked its entrance. The tiger asked a flower to roll away the stone and this rock moved, and the tiger went in, and the rock moved back."

Again his comrades shouted with laughter, then one challenged, "Beat *that* if you can!"

"Believe this or not," another hunter replied, "but in this tumbledown forest I found a tumbledown orchard; and in this tumbledown orchard I found a tumbledown house; and in this tumbledown house I found a tumbledown chest; and in this tumbledown chest I found – *this*!" And out of his hunting pouch he pulled a strip of rotting linen with a fringe of tarnished gold.

"Well tried!" cried his comrades, shouting with laughter again.

But one of them stretched out his hand for the strip of linen. He held it to the firelight to examine it, as Bona had done when Marigold first came to her. He rose and went to the king, and a sudden silence fell on the rest of the men.

"Sire," he said, "my wife is the queen's towel weaver. I know this pattern well. This is the fringe of a towel woven for the royal nursery. It was a fringe exactly like this that was torn off the towel the Princess Marigold's nurse brought back from the lake, the day the griffin carried Princess Marigold away."

"Marigold?" repeated the hunter who had told the story of the tiger's den. "That is the flower the tiger called to – *Marigold, Marigold, roll away the stone!*"

Everyone held their breath, awaiting the king's reply.

"We sleep here tonight," said the king.

If the sun was up early next morning, the king was earlier.

"Dig a trap for that tiger out of earshot of his den," he ordered his hunters. "Snare him alive and unharmed, and take him back to his den." Then he said to the huntsman who had found the cave, "Now lead me to this den."

The huntsman did so, then led the king's horse away while the king hid in a nearby tree from which he could watch the mouth of the cave. For a while nothing happened; no one went in, no one came out. Then, as day followed dawn, the rock at the cave mouth moved. Out came the tiger and it stood waiting and watching while behind it the rock moved back again.

The tiger sniffed the air, and smelled the good smell of the goat the hunters had tethered in their trap as bait. He paced towards it, advancing through his forest like a lord.

When he had passed out of earshot, the king came down from the tree, and stood before the cave. Making his voice like a tiger's – at least, as far as he was able – he called out, "Marigold, Marigold, roll away the stone!"

The stone was rolled away. The king went in.

The young girl who stood before him was so like his queen in her own girlhood that his heart leaped. But there was one difference: between her eyebrows shone a beauty spot like a tiny marigold, which had given his long-lost daughter her name.

Marigold, trembling a little at the sight of a human instead of Uncle Tiger, snatched her hazel wand from her belt and pointed it at him. Then, as she met his eyes, memory and joy flashed up in her own, and she flew into his arms like a bird.

The king's horse was led to the mouth of the cave. The king was just lifting Marigold into the saddle when the hunters hauled the tiger back, snarling but unharmed, on a strong leash. As soon as he saw Marigold on horseback, the tiger snapped his leash as if it were made of cobweb and bounded up to her, his whiskers all on end.

"Where she goes, I go," he growled. "Or who will she have to take care of her?"

The king nodded. And so, seated before her father on his horse, with her father's arm around her, her hazel wand safe in her belt, and her Uncle Tiger pacing majestically beside her, Marigold went home.

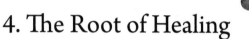

4. The Root of Healing

The forest doctor was a hare called Dr Bobtail, but all the animals called him Dr Bob. He could cure every forest sickness under the sun but then, all at once, his forest cures stopped working – just like that.

Two of his largest patients, a lion and a bear, put their heads together about it.

"The whole forest is going to bed, sick," said Leonardo-Leonides. (He was the lion.) "Look at Ursula here; she has been a bear-with-a-sore-head for months."

"And look at Leonardo's mane," added Ursula Bruin. (She was the bear.) "It keeps coming out in pawfuls. He will soon be as bald as a bone."

"If anyone can save the forest," said Dr Bob, twitching his whiskers in his gravest bedside manner, "it will be Mafanda. Let's go and see if she will."

Mafanda was the head forester's young daughter, and a great friend of all the forest beasts. She and her puppy Thomasina listened with round eyes (and Thomasina with one ear up as well) while Dr Bob told them how his

44

forest cures had suddenly stopped working, just like that.

"What made them stop?" asked Mafanda.

"My Root of Healing died," Dr Bob explained. "And without a pinch of that in it, how *can* a forest cure work?"

"Couldn't you get another?" Mafanda suggested.

"Only from the Castle of the Night," Dr Bob told her. "And only with help from the stars."

"I have a cousin forty-two times removed who lives in the Zodiac," remarked Leonardo-Leonides. "I'm sure Cousin Leo would help us, if only I could get up to him."

"And I have a great-uncle living near the Pole Star," said Ursula Bruin. "I am only a poor relation, but I feel sure Uncle Ursa Major would help us, too, if only I could get up to him."

"My mother told me," confided the puppy Thomasina, thumping her tail on the grass, "that Sirius the Dog Star is my great-great-grandpapa. I could ask *him* to help us, if only I could get up to him."

"But how would you keep the new Root of Healing alive if you got it, Dr Bob?" Mafanda asked.

"The Hare in the Moon is a distant relative of mine," replied Dr Bob, "and he knows the secret of keeping things alive. I'm sure he would advise me, if only I could get up to him."

"I could take you all in my sleep ship," offered Mafanda.

"Oh, Mafanda, it is far too small," yelped Thomasina. "That round bone box you keep it in is no bigger than your head!"

"And didn't your mother tell you, Thomasina," Mafanda teased her, "what happens to a sleep ship as soon as it is dark?"

As soon as it was dark, Mafanda took out her tiny sleep ship from its round bone box; and at once it began to grow. It grew and it grew; it grew in every direction at once till there was room for them all in it, and elbow and tail room, too.

They all lay down on its deck. A gentle wind puffed out its sail, and away they glided, slowly, smoothly, across the Sea of Quiet Breathing, under the shadow of the Hills of Slumber, and into the vast Ocean of the Sky.

In this ocean's calm blue waters, the stars lay scattered like small golden islands. A larger silver island floated among them, the full moon. On its shore stood the Hare in the Moon, stirring a bubbling brew of heavenly herbs with a silver spoon as tall as himself.

"Cousin Moon," called Dr Bob, "how can the Root of Healing stay alive on the earth?"

"Plant it in moss from a millpond, Cousin Bobtail," replied the Hare in the Moon, stirring hard. "Keep it fresh with south-running water, scooped up against the flow of the stream. Feed it with the yellow star jelly that falls from the clouds. Let the sun shine on it, let the four winds blow on it, and it will stay alive."

The sleep ship sailed on between the golden islands to the home of Ursa Major, the Great Bear. He was just setting out with his wagon and horses for a leisurely drive around the Pole Star.

"Great-uncle Ursa," called Ursula Bruin, "how do you get into the Castle of the Night?"

"Knock three times on its outer gate with a star whip, Grand-niece Ursula," the Great Bear replied. "You had better have mine." And he handed her his star whip.

The sleep ship threaded its way between the golden islands to the great Zoo Circle, the Zodiac. Here the mighty Leo was lying, crunching the crusty, fresh-baked loaves that lay heaped between his paws.

"Cousin Leo," called Leonardo-Leonides, "where in the Castle of the Night do you find the Root of Healing?"

"By the well in the inner garden, Cousin Leonardo-Leonides," Leo told him. "Two cousins of ours guard the garden door; but they will let you pass if you give them each a star loaf. You had better take two of mine." And he handed him two star loaves.

The sleep ship sailed on further till it came to an island shaped like a boat. Sirius the Dog Star stood like a captain at its prow, keeping his blue-white star watch.

"Great-great-grandpapa," called Thomasina, "if you get into the Castle of the Night, how do you get out?"

"Be out by the last stroke of midnight, dear great-great-grandchild," Sirius told her. "You had better have my star watch." And he handed her his star watch.

On they sailed, and at last they reached the Castle of the Night. Its walls came right to the water's edge and little blue waves lapped dreamily against its outer gate.

Ursula Bruin stood up in the sleep ship and knocked three times with Ursa Major's whip. The gate swung open. Out of the sleep ship they stepped, and in they all went.

On the far side of the wide courtyard two lions guarded

a door. Leonardo-Leonides gave them each a loaf, and both lay quietly down to crunch them. The door behind them swung open, and in they all went.

They came into a garden growing around a well. It was full of green and fragrant Roots of Healing. Thomasina began to dig up the nearest one with frantic nose and paws, while her tail wagged furiously. Mafanda stood over her with the star watch in her hand, her eyes fixed on the shining minute finger that was slowly creeping upright.

"*One!*" struck the star watch.

"Run!" shrieked Mafanda.

While the star watch went on striking, Dr Bob scooped up the root, and back he loped like lightning. Back sprang Leonardo-Leonides. Back raced Mafanda. Back bounded Thomasina. Back, last of all, lolloped Ursula Bruin. "*Twelve!*" struck the star watch, and the outer gate shut on her tail hairs with a clap and a clash and a clang.

The breeze from that clap-clash-and-clang blew them all aboard the sleep ship; it blew the sleep ship clean across the Ocean of the Sky and past the Hills of Slumber, over the Sea of Quiet Breathing and back to the shore of earth.

And all of a sudden it was tomorrow morning. The sleep ship had shrunk and folded its sails, and Mafanda had laid it away in its round bone box, no bigger than her head.

Together they planted the new Root of Healing in moss from a millpond. They kept it fresh with south-running water, scooped up against the flow of the stream. They fed it with the yellow star jelly that falls from the clouds. They let the sun shine on it, they let the four winds blow on it, and they kept it alive.

From then on, Dr Bob put a pinch of it in all his forest cures, and soon they cured every forest sickness under the sun again – just like that.

5. The Prince Who Lost
His Shadow

The king of a kingdom died suddenly, leaving an only son, Prince Pio, to become king next. But before Prince Pio could do this, he lost his one and only shadow.

And this is how he lost his shadow.

Prince Pio had a stepmother, the queen, and although Prince Pio didn't know it, this stepmother was a witch. This witch had a black cat named Maulkin, and although Prince Pio didn't know it, this black cat was his stepmother's companion.

The day after the old king was buried, the queen whipped Maulkin and sent her running widdershins around the church. *Widdershins* means the way the sun would go if it went backwards; witches are fond of this way, for it brings natural laws into disorder and helps them to work bad magic.

"Quick, Pio!" the queen shouted as if she were panic-stricken. "Catch Maulkin! It is forbidden for a cat to go running around a church."

So Prince Pio, who was well brought up and therefore

obedient, ran around the church after Maulkin, and he was in such a hurry that he never noticed that he was running widdershins, which is a very dangerous way to run, for then your shadow falls behind you.

Now if a witch can step on your shadow while you are running widdershins around a church, she can tug it right away from you. And this is exactly what the queen did with Prince Pio's shadow, so that when he came back to her with Maulkin spitting and scratching and cursing in his arms, he was without his one and only shadow.

"Alas and alack, my son!" cried the queen, making her eyes big and round as if with alarm. "What *have* you been doing? You have lost your one and only shadow!"

Prince Pio felt himself all over and looked all around for his shadow, but of course he could not find it, for the witch had folded it up as small and neat as a postage stamp and was holding it hidden in her palm.

"I feel just the same," he said. "Does it matter?"

"Matter?" she cried. "Of course it matters. By our old Celtic law a king must be perfect in every part, so you can't become king if you have no shadow. Go and search for it. *I* will look after the kingdom while you are away."

"If I am going hunting, I had better be dressed for hunting," thought Prince Pio. So he put on thick brown leather hunting boots and a thick old green leather hunting jacket, and set off to find his one and only shadow.

His shadow was, in fact, gripped between Maulkin's teeth as she flew through the air on her way to an Arabian sorcerer who lived in a castle on an island far across the sea. The sorcerer and

51

the queen had a wicked plan to steal Prince Pio's kingdom for themselves, and getting hold of his shadow was the first step.

Meanwhile, Prince Pio went on walking till he reached the sea, which stopped him walking any further. The sun was just going down. The seashore was deserted except for one old fisherman, who was painting a big, bold, blue eye on the front of his little white boat. His green jersey, patched all over, had a hole under the right arm.

"Prides of lions be in your path!" he greeted Prince Pio. In their kingdom, that was the polite way to greet a hunter.

"And shoals of fishes in yours," Prince Pio greeted him back. In their kingdom, that was the polite way to return a fisherman's greeting.

"This would be a fine jersey," said the fisherman, straightening up, "if only it had a patch under this arm. I don't suppose you have a spare patch, do you?"

"Only pockets made from patches," said the prince. "Take one, you're welcome to it."

The old fisherman pulled off one of Prince Pio's patch pockets and held it over the hole under his arm. It melted into the jersey as if it belonged.

"Ah!" said the old fisherman gleefully. "Now I can give my boat's weather eye such a bright blue iris that she will be able to find her own way wherever she has to go."

"Could she find her way to my shadow?" asked Prince Pio. "Did you notice I had lost it?"

"I did. She could. She shall," said the old fisherman. He licked his brush to a fine point and dipped it in black paint. He painted the last curled eyelash and stepped back to admire it. Then he washed his brush in a rock pool and dried it on the princely patch under his arm.

"Jump in, curl up and go to sleep," he said. "With her weather eye open, my boat can travel both by daylight and by starlight as sure and straight as a bird."

"And when she gets there, wherever *there* is?" Prince Pio asked.

"Pull her up on dry land and turn her weather eye seaward," the old fisherman told him. "There she will wait like a faithful old dog to bring you and your shadow home. Aye, and more than your shadow, if what my new patch whispers turns out to be true."

Prince Pio, being well brought up and therefore obedient, jumped in, curled up and went to sleep. He did not wake as the boat rocked over the waves behind its bright blue weather eye. He did not wake when dusk fell. He did not wake when dusk deepened into dark. He did not wake till the prow jarred on a shingle beach. Then, he opened his eyes to see, high above him, a lighted castle jutting on a black and silver sky and blotting out the stars.

"Well," thought Prince Pio, "here I am, I know not where, nor how I am to find my shadow in wherever it is I am. Still, kill or cure, end or mend, up to this castle I must wend."

He pulled the boat up on dry land and turned her weather eye seaward. Up, up, up through the night he climbed over shingle and rocks to the tall castle, and scarcely had he reached its torch-lit courtyard when two red lights like balls of fire rushed down out of the sky towards him.

As he hid in the shadows, the lights turned into cat's

eyes. Then who should land neatly on her four black feet in that torch-lit courtyard but Maulkin! And who should step lightly down from Maulkin's back but Prince Pio's stepmother, very queenly in her scarlet mantle and her golden crown!

Now, Prince Pio was a dear, good, simple soul who never thought bad things about anyone. So, although their method of air travel made him scratch his head, he was just about to greet his stepmother warmly when the door of the castle swung open; and out stalked the Arabian sorcerer, tall and gaunt in his long black gown, his bald skull enclosed in a round black cap studded with gems, to welcome her. And his stepmother's first words made Prince Pio think twice about shouting out.

"Have you fastened my stepson's shadow to his puppet?" she asked.

"I have," the sorcerer nodded.

"And are they both being looked after by a pure and noble captive girl?" she asked again.

Again the sorcerer nodded. "All I need is your help," he said, "to bring the puppet to life. Then we can send it out at once to do such bad things in your stepson's name that the kingdom will be glad for us to rule it."

The queen lifted her head and sniffed the air. "By the pricking of my thumbs," she said, "he is already on his way here. So let's go inside and blast him to death with a whirlwind."

They went into the castle, Maulkin slinking between them, and the door closed with a clang behind them. But almost at once it burst open and, with a terrible shrieking, a whirlwind tore across the courtyard, blowing the torches into writhing ribbons of fire, and plunged down into the sea.

In the dark, Prince Pio could hear the roar of the churning waves as they piled up into mountains, then dashed themselves to foam on the rocks below. If he'd been out on that lashing, crashing sea, he would certainly never have lived to tell the tale.

Then suddenly, above the tumult, he heard a sweet voice singing, and the fury of the storm and the whirlwind died gently away. As if by magic, the full moon stood clear and bright in heaven. As if by magic, the sea slept peacefully beneath its light. Seals lay on the rocks, enraptured by the singing, and fishes lifted their heads from the still water, mouths open with delight.

Prince Pio slipped around the castle till, craning his head backward, he saw, far above, the lighted window from which the singing came. Leaning from it, framed in its light, were the head and shoulders of a girl.

Hand over hand and foot above foot, he climbed the stout ivy up the castle wall till he reached the open casement window.

"Oh!" the girl cried. "You are safe, you are safe, Prince Pio! The whirlwind did not blast you!"

She drew him into the room. "I am Phao," she told him. "The sorcerer holds me captive, for the presence of a girl gives power to his spells. But, as you just saw, where I can I work to undo his evil enchantments."

"But why have you never climbed down the ivy and escaped?" he cried.

"There was no boat," she said. "Witches and sorcerers have swifter ways of travelling."

"There is a boat now," he whispered, taking her hand. Then, suddenly remembering, he exclaimed, "You called me by my name! How did you know?"

"Come and see," she said. Taking up the silver lamp lit the room, Phao led Prince Pio to a shadowy corner. He jumped when he saw what the light revealed. For there, asleep on a small bed, lay himself!

And yet, as he stared, he shuddered. "Am I really like that?" he gasped.

"It is a most lying likeness," Phao comforted him. "For all that is good in you has here been turned to evil. And yet it still looks like you. That is how I knew you were Prince Pio, for I heard the sorcerer chant your name when he fastened your shadow to your puppet."

"I've come for my shadow," he told her. "If I don't get it back before my stepmother and the sorcerer bring this puppet to life, a lot of evil things will happen in the world."

"I will help you," said Phao.

She held the lamp so that the prince's lost shadow slid away from the puppet till it was fastened only at the feet.

"Pull! Pull hard," she cried.

Prince Pio grasped his shadow and pulled hard. It stood firm, but then all at once it quivered. It tore free and leaped to him and was his own again. And as this happened, the shape and the features of the puppet melted like mist, and on the bed lay only a formless block of wood.

Phao and Prince Pio could hear voices coming from the

spiral staircase that led up to Phao's tower. The sorcerer and the queen were coming.

"They're coming to bring the puppet to life," Phao whispered. "Quick, or we shall be too late."

She blew out the lamp and they went head first out of the casement window, and down the ivy like lightning. They were running hand in hand from the courtyard towards the beach when a tornado burst out of the castle and tossed them into the air like straws.

"They are raising a new whirlwind against us," gasped Phao. "I must send it back to them."

And again, most sweetly, she began to sing.

The whirlwind dropped them to the ground and whirled its way back to the castle. As they picked each other up and ran, they heard it batter down the doors. From the inner halls they heard clap after clap of thunder.

Together they pushed the boat down the beach to the edge of the tide and jumped in. Winking its weather eye, the boat skimmed off like a gull across the quiet water.

Looking back at the tall castle looming in the moonlight, they saw the courtyard torches spin and dive in the blasts of the whirlwind. They saw the broken walls gaping with holes; they saw flames that shot sky-high. Then the castle tottered and crashed among the flames with a mighty bang that shook the island.

But King Pio, under a sky growing pale with the coming dawn, was safe in the boat. He smiled as he swiftly and joyfully took his new queen, and his shadow, home.

6. The Unicorn's Fosterling

There was once, I am not sure when, in a far land, I am not sure where, a wizard skilled in every sort of sorcery. The more he got, the more he wanted, and the more he wanted, the more he got, till at last he said, "There isn't a thing in life left to want, except not to die!"

He went into the desert, and drew symbols in the sand. The symbols shifted and shaped themselves into a secret script.

"The person," he read, "who carries within them the sun and the ruby of Amfortas, will never die."

Now the wizard knew where to find the sun any day of the week, but he did not know where to find the ruby of Amfortas. So he put himself into a magic sleep, and sent himself out to find it.

He travelled back through the years – how far, who can say? – till he found a wounded king, King Amfortas, in a castle on Mount Salvat. On his head was a fur cap with bands of Arabian gold woven into it. And on the top of the cap flashed a ruby.

The wizard watched how the cap decayed as the years went by, till at last the ruby fell from its frayed setting. He saw how the ruby was reset into a carved Spanish comb. He saw the comb passed down from mother to daughter, its story gradually forgotten, till all its wearer knew was that she must never lose it, or bad things would happen to the world.

The wearer of the comb was a young Spanish girl, called Señorita Serenita (for she was as happy as the day is long). The wizard saw the ruby gleam in her smoothly piled black hair as she moved in and out of the sunlit courtyard of the little house below Mount Salvat in which she lived alone.

The wizard was a mighty shape shifter. He had only to think like any bird or beast, and he *was* that bird or beast. So he thought like a carrion crow, and he *was* a carrion crow. Away he flew, over the desert, over the sea, over the orange groves of Spain, to land in the sunny courtyard of Señorita Serenita.

It was midday, so everyone was asleep, as is the custom in Spain. Señorita Serenita, taking her siesta in the cool shade of a leafy orange tree by the high wall of the courtyard, did not feel the wizard's bony beak pull the carved comb from her hair, and did not see it peck the ruby out of its setting and shut with a snap as the scrawny throat gulped it down.

Nor did she see the carrion crow hide her comb in his feathers, spread his wide black wings, and fly away towards the south. But when she woke up and went to tidy her hair, she found her comb was missing.

To and fro she ran, crying like a fountain, wringing her hands, searching the stones of the courtyard, shaking the orange tree branches, and moaning to herself, "Oh no, oh no, Serenita! What bad things will happen to the world because you've lost the comb?"

The carrion crow flew for the rest of that day – south over the orange groves of Spain, south over the sea, then east over the desert, east over forests, east over mountains, and east over plains.

The day waned, and the night waxed. Still he flew on, under black sky and brilliant stars, till, just as the first cockerels were crowing, he came to the eastern shore of the World's End.

Out of his dark wisdom the wizard knew that only one creature in all the world could swallow the sun: the wolf. At each eclipse of the sun he had watched the same drama – the sun fleeing, the world pursuing, the wolf swallowing, the world darkening. But the sun was always too strong for the wolf, and, burning him to ashes, burst forth again in splendour.

So the carrion crow thought like a wolf, and he *was* a wolf, the carved comb clinging to his fur. Then he thought of himself dressed in iron, and he *was* an iron wolf, who could conquer the sun with the strongest of metals. The comb slipped off the iron, and fell to the sand.

As the sun came slowly up out of the sea, staining the sky with rose, the iron wolf, opening iron jaws, sprang at the sun and gulped it down. The rosy sky grew grey. The birds ceased their dawn chorus between one note and the next. Twilight fell on the whole world.

On the eastern shore of the World's End lived Fosterling the Faun, with his foster father, a white unicorn. Just as night was waning and day was waxing he always woke, for he loved to greet his friend the sun as it rose out of the sea. But today, before he had time to greet it, his friend vanished, and day waned again.

Now a faun, as anyone who has ever met one knows, is just like any other boy except for the tiny horns among the curls of his hair. So, just as any other boy would do if his friend vanished before his eyes, he shook his foster father awake.

"Wake up, Father Unicorn!" he cried. "Friend Sun has vanished!"

Now a unicorn, as anyone who has ever met one knows, is just like any other white horse except for the long horn growing out of his brow. This horn is so sharp that there is no substance it cannot pierce; and it gives the unicorn power to see anything he looks for, all the wide world over.

So now Father Unicorn looked for the sun, and as soon as he looked for it, he found it.

"An iron wolf has eaten Friend Sun," he reported, "together with the biggest ruby in the world."

"Can we get them back?" asked Fosterling, running anxiously to and fro at the edge of the sea.

"Only with the help," said Father Unicorn, "of the owner of the ruby."

Fosterling tripped as he ran, and stooped to pick up what had tripped him. It was Señorita Serenita's comb.

"What *is* this?" he asked. "I have never seen one before."

For, as anyone who has ever met one knows, neither fauns nor unicorns as a rule wear combs in their hair.

"It is a comb, a Spanish one," Father Unicorn told him. "Ladies wear them in their hair. Look, Fosterling, there is a hole in it where a huge gem has been! If that gem was this ruby, it must have come from Spain."

As soon as he looked for Spain, he found Spain. As soon as he looked in Spain for the owner of the ruby, he found the owner of the ruby. He found her running to and fro, weeping like a fountain, wringing her hands, searching the stones of her courtyard, shaking her orange tree branches, and all the time moaning to herself, "Oh no, oh no, Serenita! When you lost the ruby of Amfortas, what bad things have happened to the world!"

"Get up, Fosterling!" ordered Father Unicorn. "Put the comb in your curls!"

Fosterling climbed onto Father Unicorn's back, the comb in his yellow curls, and with grey twilight all around them, Father Unicorn set off. They left behind the eastern shore of the World's End. They left behind the plains. They left behind the mountains. They left behind the forests. And at last, in the same grey twilight, they came to the edge of the desert.

"Fosterling," ordered Father Unicorn, "tear out my horn!"

"I would rather die first," said Fosterling.

"And *then* how will you rescue Friend Sun?" Father Unicorn asked him.

So Fosterling did it, sadly. A mist arose round Father

Unicorn, and within the mist a flame. When the mist and the flame had passed, there was no unicorn, but instead a noble black horse with a streaming mane.

"Fosterling," said the black horse, "always obey your elders; they have lived longer than you. The scorpions in this desert sting unicorns to death, but a black horse is safe from them. Get up Fosterling, and hold the unicorn horn in your right hand!"

Fosterling climbed onto Father Unicorn's back, the comb in his yellow curls, the unicorn horn in his right hand; and with grey twilight all around them, the black horse set off. They left the desert behind them and came to the edge of the sea.

"Fosterling," ordered the black horse, "cut off my mane!"

"I would rather die first," said Fosterling.

"And *then* how will you rescue Friend Sun?" the black horse asked him.

So Fosterling did it, sadly. A mist arose round the black horse, and within the mist a flame. When the mist and the flame had passed, there was no black horse, but instead Pegasus stood there, pawing the sand, his great wings beating like a butterfly.

"Fosterling," said Pegasus, "always obey your elders; they have lived longer than you. Only a winged horse can carry you over the sea. Get up Fosterling, and hold the black mane in your left hand!"

Fosterling climbed onto Pegasus's back, the comb in his yellow curls, the unicorn horn in his right hand, the black horse's mane in his left; and with grey twilight all around them, Pegasus flew up into the air. They left behind the sea, and they left behind the orange groves of Spain, and came to the foot of Mount Salvat.

There they found Señorita Serenita, moaning to herself, "Oh no, oh no, Serenita! How can you heal the world when so many bad things have happened?"

"We are here to take you to heal it," Pegasus told her.

Fosterling took her comb from his yellow curls and held it out to her. She put the comb in her own black locks, and climbed onto Pegasus's back, behind Fosterling. With grey twilight all around them, they left behind the orange groves, they left behind the sea, they left behind the desert, the forests, the mountains, the plains, and they came to the eastern shore of the World's End.

"Fosterling," ordered Pegasus, "drown me!"

"I would rather die first," said Fosterling.

"And *then* how will you rescue Friend Sun?" Pegasus asked him.

So Fosterling did it, sadly. Pegasus sank under the waves. A mist arose above him, and within the mist a flame. When the mist and the flame had passed, there was no Pegasus, but instead, out of the waves, rose a golden eagle.

"Fosterling," said the golden eagle, "always obey your elders; they have lived longer than you. Only an eagle can look Friend Sun full in the face. Get up, both of you! Bind yourselves to my back with the black horse's mane. Fosterling, give Señorita Serenita the unicorn horn, for only she can free Friend Sun and the ruby of Amfortas."

With Fosterling and Señorita Serenita bound firmly to his

back, grey twilight all around him, the golden eagle flew out to a rock in the sea where the iron wolf crouched. It was howling in agony.

"Save me! Save me!" he howled. "Save me from this sun that burns and blazes in me!"

Señorita Serenita leaned from the golden eagle's back, with her left hand holding on to Fosterling's shoulder. In her right hand was the unicorn horn, so sharp that there was no substance it could not pierce. She drove it into the iron wolf, exactly where her comb had rested.

As she did that, out burst Friend Sun, so blinding bright that Fosterling and Señorita Serenita hid their eyes in the golden eagle's feathers; so blinding bright that they would have fallen with the shock of so much splendour had they not been safely bound with the black horse's mane.

But the golden eagle stared at Friend Sun undazzled, watching for the ruby of Amfortas to follow out of the wolf. He caught it in his beak, just before it fell into the sea. The iron wolf, breathing his last breath, howling his last howl, slid from the rock and the waves closed over him as if he had never been.

Friend Sun began to climb up into the sky. The birds took up their dawn chorus just where they had left off; the grey twilight waned, and warmth and light and colour waxed till they flooded the whole world.

Back on the eastern shore, at the very spot where Fosterling had tripped over the comb, the beak of the golden eagle reset the great ruby the carrion crow's beak had pecked out.

"Fosterling," said the golden eagle, "always obey your elders; they have lived longer than you. You had better marry Señorita Serenita and help her to guard her ruby, and be as happy as the day is long again."

So Fosterling did it, joyfully.

7. The Gorgeous Nightingale

King Magnus had a baby daughter, Princess Betula-Alba and, as was usual, twelve godmothers came to the princess's christening. One by one they came to the golden cradle with their life gifts: she would grow up gentle and kind; she would be as graceful as the silver birch tree; she would marry a boy as clear and precious as a gemstone of jasper.

The second-to-last godmother laid a tiny crystal bottle in the princess' tiny hand. It held the rainbow spark of a dewdrop. As she did so, the door burst open, and in stamped an old crone as hideous as a nightmare.

"I see the princess has the Dewdrop of Life," she croaked. "But she will only throw it away!"

And out she stamped again, banging the door behind her, so that the tapestries on the stone walls blew around with the gust of wind, while the christening guests stared at each other with eyes as big as saucers.

The last godmother of all stepped forward. "She *will* throw it away," she said, "but in doing so she will save her father from the worst of deaths."

The queen took care of the crystal bottle till Betula-Alba grew up. Then she had a golden locket made to hold it, shaped like a heart, and when Betula-Alba was old enough, she hung it on a golden chain around the child's neck, telling her to wear the heart of gold day and night, next to her own.

The very next morning Betula-Alba was wakened early by bird song in the wood beyond the palace gardens. She left her bed and went lightly over the dewy grass to the wood. Just as the sun came over the edge of the world, broad and red and glorious, she saw a shepherd boy standing under a silver birch tree, his flock of sheep close and quiet around him.

He stood in a brown cloud of small birds, all singing their small hearts out, while larks dropped out of the sky in singing spirals to join them. The shepherd boy gazed at the princess, and the princess gazed at the shepherd boy – and she did not need to be told that his name was Jasper.

She went that morning to her father's throne room. He sat on his hard golden throne, wearing his hard golden crown.

"Father," she said, "I have found the boy as clear and precious as jasper! He is a shepherd boy."

"A shepherd boy?" thundered King Magnus. "When a nightingale is as gorgeous as a peacock, then and only then shall my daughter marry a shepherd boy!" And he had the shepherd boy shut up in a tower in the middle of a lake, with water in every direction as far as the eye could see.

That night, as Betula-Alba lay awake, she heard a nightingale singing. She went out into the moonlight, and stood under his branch. She told him where Jasper was, and begged him to go and sing to him, to comfort him in his loneliness.

Away flew the nightingale, over field and fell and moor and mountain, to the tower in the lake. He landed on the ivy near a slit in the thick stone wall, sipped a drop of dew from an ivy leaf to clear his throat, and then lifted up his small brown head and sang.

In his dark dungeon, Jasper stood chained to a pillar. His head hung low onto his chest, and the heart in that chest was heavy. Suddenly, rising triumphantly above the wailing of the wind and the lapping of water on stone, came the first rich notes of the song of a nightingale. Jasper lifted his head and turned his eyes to the moonlit slit, and felt comforted in his heart.

When the birds that greet the sun awoke and drank their drops of dew to clear their throats, the nightingale was still singing. From all parts of the kingdom, over field and fell and moor and mountain, his song drew them to the tower in the lake, till you couldn't see any stone or ivy because they were covered in small brown birds.

And as the sun came over the edge of the world, broad and red and glorious, they greeted it with such a noise that Jasper forgot his captivity, and even his warders crowded to the arrow-slits, open-mouthed, to listen.

They sent a message to King Magnus to tell him of this invasion of singing birds, and the next night he had his servants row him out to the tower in his royal barge. Again the nightingale came and sang, and again, at dawn, clouds of other birds flew to sing with him.

King Magnus thought as he listened, "I am not *really* harsh and cruel; my true self is quite different. If I can get this nightingale to sing to *me*, all these other birds will join him and that will *show* how gentle and kind I really am at heart."

So he had the nightingale caught and put into a golden cage, and he had the golden cage hung in his throne room. Then he came in, in his royal robes and his golden crown, and, sitting on his golden throne, he barked out, "Sing, nightingale!"

The nightingale shrank away from the king, as far as his cage would let him. His heart beat wildly, but he did not sing one note.

"Sing, nightingale!" King Magnus barked again.

Still the nightingale sat huddled in his corner, and still he did not sing one note.

King Magnus strode to the golden cage and shook his fist at the nightingale.

"Sing! For the last time, sing, nightingale!" he shouted. "Sing, or your neck shall be wrung, and you shall be plucked and roasted and served up tonight at my table!"

But the nightingale still huddled in his corner, and still didn't sing a single note.

King Magnus threw his crown on the throne-room floor, denting it rather badly, and flung open the door, bellowing for his cook to fetch the nightingale. The cook came and took away the nightingale in his golden cage.

Betula-Alba heard the king's bellow far away in the wood. She ran across the gardens and burst into the throne room.

"What is it, Father?" she asked. "Were you talking about *my* nightingale? Where is he?"

"In the kitchen," King Magnus snapped.

Betula-Alba flew like a bird. In the palace kitchen the golden cage stood empty, and on a roasting pan beside it, already plucked, lay the nightingale.

Betula-Alba cried out, and grasped the golden locket that lay on her own heart. She had taken out the tiny crystal bottle and unscrewed its silver stopper, and was just tipping out the dewdrop, when in strode King Magnus and roughly caught her wrist.

"That dewdrop is to save *me* from death!" he stormed. "How dare you throw it away?"

"Isn't that what it was foretold I *would* do, Father?" asked Betula-Alba.

And she twisted her wrist in his iron grip, so that the Dewdrop of Life fell, *splash,* on the dead, naked nightingale.

Then the nightingale stood up in the roasting pan, only flesh and bones; and he lifted up his stringy throat and sang. Betula-Alba swooped and cupped him in her hands, and out she ran with him, still singing, across the palace gardens to Jasper's silver birch tree.

At the call of that song, birds came flocking till you could not see Betula-Alba's golden dress for birds. Then she opened her hands and showed them the naked nightingale, and asked if each could spare him just one feather to help clothe him.

What a delicious chirping and chirruping broke out then, as each bird, preening and sleeking his feathers, called on his neighbours to help him choose his best and most beautiful one!

Now there was a flying queue to Betula-Alba's shoulder, a feather in each bird's beak. The robins brought red ones from their breasts, the chaffinches white ones from their wings, the golden-crested wrens yellow ones from their crowns, to make a new crown for the nightingale. There were black ones from the blackbirds, blue ones from the jays, green ones from the woodpeckers, iris ones from the doves, and all the browns under the sun from the small brown birds.

Each feather fastened itself on the nightingale's nakedness as if guided by an invisible needle, till Betula-Alba called joyfully to the birds, "Bravo! You have made our little nightingale as gorgeous as a peacock!"

Her own words rang in her ears as if someone else's voice had said them, and the memory they evoked shook a surge of hope within her. She hid the gorgeous nightingale under her arm and ran back across the gardens, bursting into the throne room like a happy wind.

King Magnus was sitting alone on his throne, wearing his dented crown, looking, truth to tell, a little lonely and pathetic. Betula-Alba laid a gentle hand on his arm.

"Father, *when* did you say I could marry Jasper?" she asked him, her face shining.

"When a nightingale is as gorgeous as a peacock," he snapped, "and I meant it, every word."

Betula-Alba laughed a laugh of purest joy as she drew the many-coloured nightingale from under her arm.

"That is no nightingale!" King Magnus barked, scowling at this vision of miniature splendour. "If he is, let him sing!"

The nightingale stood up on Betula-Alba's palm. He spread out his rainbow plumage and perkily tipped his golden feather crown towards the king's golden dented one, lifted his iridescent little throat, and sang.

King Magnus nodded, knowing at once this was truly a nightingale, for the sweet pangs of a nightingale's song can melt a heart of stone. His own heart melted as he listened, and he suddenly saw how near his own best self had come to being slain by pride and cruelty. He put his arm around Betula-Alba and drew her to him.

"The last godmother was right – you have saved me from the worst of deaths," he said. "Quick, send for Jasper, and you shall marry him here and now!"

Every bird in the kingdom came to that wedding feast. They took crumbs of wedding cake from the lips of bride and bridegroom, and sipped hydromel (which is honey wine) to make their throats clear, and sang as they had never sung before; but the sweetest singer of them all was the gorgeous nightingale.

And from that day King Magnus, with all his fire and force, became a truly great king.

8. The King's Candle

There was once an island kingdom that had only one harbour. Steep cliffs, so steep that no one could climb them, protected it everywhere else. The city built around the harbour was guarded by sturdy sea walls. And it was in this city that the king had his palace.

In the middle of the palace was the king's room; in the middle of the king's room was the king's bed; at the head of the king's bed was the king's candle.

The king's candle was made of the purest beeswax. It stood thicker than his body and taller than his head, and its wick was a bunch of rushes too big to be grasped by two hands. The candle never burned out, except when the king died. Then, the king's candle would be relit by a spear whose blazing head was kept in a tall jade jar filled with water. All the sons of the dead king had to walk past the candle, and as the one who would be the next king passed by, the spear sprang out of the water and lit the candle from its own blazing tip.

When the king's candle went out, every light in the kingdom, every fire in the kingdom, would also go out with it. Frantically, the people would come running to the palace, each with a wax taper clasped in one palm and a copper coin clasped in the other, to buy new light, new fire, from the new king's candle. For this was the custom in those days and in that kingdom.

Strung on the spear's shaft were fifty clashing rings of gold, and hung on the rings were five hundred clashing bells of silver. As the spear came to life to relight the candle, the golden rings and silver bells would clang and clash, letting everyone know that fire and candlelight had come back to the land. And the people would rejoice, shouting, "The king is dead. Long live the king!"

One day, the king of this kingdom died. Out went his candle; out went every light and every fire, all over the island. The people came running, a taper in one hand and a copper coin in the other. The crowd in front of the palace was so dense that a fly could not have edged its way between them.

The dead king didn't have any children, but his brother had seven sons. The king's wise man sent for these princes, to walk past the king's candle. One by one they passed by, but the spear stayed still, its head in the jade jar of water.

"Here is a new thing!" cried the seven princes. "What does it mean?"

"It means," said the wise man, "that none of you seven is the new king."

"Does it, indeed?" raged the eldest prince, Prince Zabulo. "We will see about that!" And he grabbed the spear from its jar, to light the king's candle himself.

The crowds outside the palace heard the clash of golden rings and silver bells and started to shout, "Long live the king!"

But no new king came out to invite them to enter and light their tapers, and soon the rumour was blowing from mouth to mouth that Prince Zabulo had grabbed the spear from its jar and its blazing head had gone out.

And so indeed it had, for, as he pulled the spear's blazing head from the water, the flame at its point went out with a pop. He held the still-glowing top to the candle's wick, but no candle flame sprang up. Instead, the spear writhed out of his hand, and like a giant quill pen guided by unseen fingers, its red tip wrote four words on the marble floor, before the spear fell with a clang. In letters of fire the words shone out:

New days, new ways.

The wise man and the seven princes watched the letters slowly fade. When they picked up the spear, its tip was already cold.

"Here is another new thing!" cried the princes. "With no spear, how shall we choose which one of us is to be king?"

"None of you is to be king," the wise man replied. "New days, new ways." And he sent heralds by swift boat to all the nearby kingdoms, to proclaim that the first prince of any land to light the king's candle would become king of this land.

From every point of the compass, royal ships sailed swiftly to the island's harbour – galleys with gilded sterns, longships with dragon prows, galleons, caravels and sashmarays. The ships were laden with lighted lamps and lanterns, with fire in braziers, buckets, boxes and even warming pans. But the moment the princes brought them ashore on the island, every light, every fire, shot out a spark and went out.

"Here is yet another new thing!" observed the seven princes, well pleased. "Old fire cannot live in our land."

But the people, who had no fires to cook their suppers and who had to go to bed these days as soon as it was dark, were not so pleased.

"A king! A king!" they roared. "Give us a new king, you wise man and you princes, or we will empty your eight bodies of your souls!"

So the wise man sent heralds by swift boat again, to proclaim that if *any* fire-maker could make new fire on the island and light the king's candle with it, he would be king, even though he didn't have a drop of royal blood in his body.

Because the king's candle had always been there, no one on the whole island knew how to make fire – and in those days, matches hadn't been invented.

Three days later, the watchmen on the sea walls sent word to the palace that a boat was approaching. The wise man came quickly, with the seven princes at his heels, and with all the people at theirs. They saw a stranger, as tall and thin as a beanpole, paddling a bark canoe into the harbour. He was wrapped in a bright blanket, and he wore dyed feathers in his hair.

"What will you make new fire with?" the wise man asked him.

"With these," said the stranger. From beneath his blanket he brought out a cylinder like a sharpened pencil and a block of wood with a cup-shaped hollow in it. "What do people pay for new light in this kingdom?" he asked.

"A copper coin from each house," the wise man told him.

"To me they shall pay a silver one," said the stranger.

The people groaned. But they had to have light and fire, so the crowd parted so the stranger could get to the palace.

In the king's room, the stranger asked the wise man to hold the block of wood steady for him. Into the hollow he set the sharpened point of the cylinder, and twirled till the wood grew hot and a faint wing of transparent flame shot up.

The princes drew in their breaths sharply, but the flame died as soon as it was born. The stranger kept twirling, but he couldn't make any more fire.

"This works in my own land," said the stranger, very perplexed. "It may be that to work here, it needs wood grown in this kingdom."

The wise man looked closely at the cylinder and the block of wood.

"We don't grow any wood on our island as hard as this cylinder," he said, "and no wood as soft as your block."

So the stranger paddled his bark canoe sadly away, and the king's candle still stood unlit.

Next day, the watchmen on the sea walls sent word to the palace that a second boat was approaching. The wise man came quickly, with the seven princes at his heels, and with all the people at theirs. They saw a stranger, as big and solid as a tower, rowing a coracle made from wicker and animal hides into the harbour. A silver shoulder-brooch held the folds of his plaid in place, and at the front of his tartan kilt hung a goatskin sporran.

"What will you make new fire with?" the wise man asked him.

"With these," said the stranger, and out of his sporran he took a flint and a meteorite. "What do people pay for new light in this kingdom?" he asked.

"A copper coin from each house," the wise man told him.

"To me they shall pay a gold one," said the stranger.

The people groaned. But they had to have light and fire, so the crowd parted so the stranger could get to the palace.

In the king's room, the stranger struck the earthly stone and the heavenly stone together. A spark leaped forth.

The princes drew in their breaths sharply. But the spark died before it fell on the tinder placed to receive it. The stranger kept striking, but he couldn't make any more sparks.

"This works in my own land," said the stranger, very perplexed. "It may be that to work here, it needs flint from your own rocks, and star iron that has fallen into your own fields."

The wise man looked closely at both the flint and the meteorite.

"We have neither of these on our island," he said.

So the stranger put the flint and the meteorite back into his sporran. He rowed his coracle sadly away, and the king's candle still stood unlit.

It was still before sunrise next day when the watchmen on the sea walls were roused by a shout from the water, and a cheerful young voice asking for permission to land.

"Can't you wait to begin your day with the sun, as other men do?" the watchmen grumbled.

"The sun and my boat are so drawn to each other," the happy young voice replied, "that I only dare sail her at night."

They gave him permission to land. Still in the dark before dawn, he wrapped the boat in its sail and begged one of the watchmen to guard it with his life.

"There is not another like it in all the seven seas," he said.

"You made it with your own hands?" the watchman asked.

"And my own mouth," the stranger added.

At sunrise the wise man came quickly, with the seven princes at his heels, and with all the people at theirs. The stranger they came to greet was a young man, barefoot and in rags, his lips twitching with laughter at the jokes he was telling himself.

"What will you make new fire with?" the wise man asked him.

"With this," said the stranger, and out of his rags he drew a transparent, colourless globe, a little like a crystal.

"And what will *you* charge the people for new light?" asked a voice from the dense crowd.

"Gutrin's candlelight shall be as free as sunlight," answered Gutrin.

The crowd cheered and shouted words of friendship as they parted so the stranger could get to the palace.

In the king's room, Gutrin opened the casement window

wide and placed the king's candle near it. Sunlight came pouring in, and he held up his colourless sphere, standing as still as a stone.

All eyes were fixed on the sphere as the sunlight streamed into it. But suddenly the wise man gave a cry. "The king's candle! The candle is lit!"

The rejoicing swept like wildfire through the palace and out to the waiting crowd. A roar of joy went up from them like the roaring of the sea. They battered open the palace doors and in they surged, tapers in hand, for their free candlelight.

But the seven princes swept Gutrin and the wise man into the king's robing chamber, and their voices were as shrill as cats in the moonlight.

"But he did nothing – nothing! Is he to be king for merely holding a jewel in the sun?"

"Unless the sun lights the candle," answered Gutrin, still smiling, "a man labours in vain to light it."

"But how did the jewel do it?" shrieked the princes.

They snatched the globe from him to see. They snatched it from one another. All in a flash, no one quite knew how, *crash*, it fell on the marble floor.

They drew apart. The transparent globe lay splintered into tiny fragments. Around the fragments spread a tiny pool.

"Then it was *not* a jewel!" Prince Zabulo accused him.

"*You* called it that, not I," smiled Gutrin. "It was a hollow sphere of glass."

"Glass? What is glass?" asked the wise man.

"A substance you can see through, made from sand,"

Gutrin told him. "That's how I got my name; Gutrin means glass in my land. You see, I am a glass blower."

"Sand," mused the wise man. "We have no sand on our island. And what was the liquid in the globe?"

"Water," said Gutrin.

"Water?" howled Prince Zabulo. "You won my uncle's throne with sand and water? No, that is too much. My sword slips very easily from its scabbard. What is to stop it from slipping now and leaving you a head shorter?"

"This," said the wise man sternly. "That when a king is every poor man's friend, every poor man is his. Touch a hair of your new king's head, and the people will tear you to tatters."

Suddenly, the sound of a horn made them all fall silent. A breathless messenger entered and knelt before the new king, who was still in his rags.

"Sire, the watchmen on the sea walls have sighted an armada," he announced. "It is sailing towards our harbour. It is the war fleet of the king who tried to conquer our land last year."

"He thinks he'll easily conquer it now with, as he thinks, no king's candle alight," said the wise man. "Sire, you must ring the war alarm and man the walls!"

"No," said King Gutrin suddenly. "He has come on a day of bright sun, and that has delivered him into our hands. We can defeat that armada without the loss of a single man."

He ran down to the harbour, wise man and princes at his heels, the people at theirs. He pulled the sail off his wrapped-up boat, and they saw it was a boat of glass, as clear and as round as a goldfish bowl.

"Fill it with water," commanded King Gutrin.

The people ran to do as he ordered.

"Now set up the crane for hurling stones at the enemy," he commanded again. "Set it up in the place I will show you. Then set my boat in it and lift it high up."

And again the people ran to do as he ordered.

"Leave the walls unmanned," he commanded.

And they did so.

The war fleet came closer. It dropped anchor just out of bowshot of the walls. The walls were deserted. No army was gathered and no ships were manned. Only a great transparent globe hung high in the air. The invading king feared a trap and sent to consult his leaders.

While they argued this way and that, the sunlight streamed into the great glass globe of water. Powerfully it focused the sun's rays upon the wooden ships. Soon smoke began to rise, then flames began to leap and lap and spread. The armada was on fire.

As King Gutrin had promised, he defeated the invaders without the loss of one man.

When the last charred and crippled ship had limped away over the skyline, King Gutrin, still in rags, turned to go back to the palace.

"Long live the king!" roared the people, pressing around him.

"Long live the king!" echoed the princes, transformed from his enemies to his friends.

And live long he did, a friend to everyone in that country.

9. Rose and Lily

There was once a king whose twin sons were as similar as two peas in a pod. When one fell sick, they both fell sick. The royal physicians racked their brains and their pharmacies, but nothing they found in either could cure the royal twins.

"Your Majesty," said the chief royal physician at last, "what did you lose just before the princes fell sick?"

"Lose?" repeated the king, slapping all the pockets in his royal robes. "Why, bless my soul, I remember now – I lost my little-finger ring."

"I thought as much," nodded the chief royal physician. "It has come into the witch-queen's hands and given her power over the princes. They will never be well again unless you get it back."

The king promised fountains of jewels and gold in a solid shower to anyone who would bring back his little-finger ring. But though many set out to find it, no one brought it back, for in her own land the witch-queen had power over earth and fire and water, and all the ways to her castle were strewn with strong enchantments.

Now the king's gardener had twin daughters, Rose and Lily.

"Lily," said Rose, "I am going to find that ring. Watch my rosebush while I am gone. If its flowers stay fresh, I'm fine; if they droop, I'm in trouble."

Off she set, over the green meadows. Though the grass was green, it grew greener where she trod, and in every footprint grew a small red rose the size of a little-finger ring.

She went a short way, she went a long way, and she came to a stream. A fish lay gasping on the bank. She put it back into the stream, and on she went.

She went a short way, she went a long way, and she came to a mill. An otter was stuck, whirling by the water wheel. She helped it back to land, and on she went.

She went a short way, she went a long way, and she came to some wild water. There was no bridge. There was no boat.

"What does it matter?" said Rose. "I can swim."

But as soon as she dipped her toes in the water, she vanished in a puff of smoke.

At that very moment, in the garden at home, Rose's rose tree began to wilt.

"*Now* where has Rose got to?" said Lily.

Off she set to find her, over the green meadows, following Rose's footprints, in every footprint a small red rose the size of a little-finger ring.

She went a short way, she went a long way, and she came to the stream; then she came to the mill; and finally she came to the wild water. The green footprints led right down into the water.

The sun was overhead. Lily lifted her arms and called aloud:

"All creatures, bird or beast,
The greatest creature, or the least,
To whom my sister has been kind,
Help me, now, Rose to find."

The fish came swimming. The otter came running.

"I will find her," said the fish.

It swam to a quiet backwater, and listened to the secrets in the whispering of the waters. Soon it swam back.

"I have found her," it said. "She is a white stone among the other white stones on the bed of the wild water, but out of her grows a small red rose the size of a little-finger ring."

"I will find her," said the otter.

The otter dived in, and a string of bubbles rose up. Then it came out, shook itself, and laid a white stone and a small red rose at Lily's feet. As soon as they touched the grass, they vanished in a puff of smoke, and there on that spot stood Rose.

"Come home with me, Rose," begged Lily.

"I have braved one danger; I can brave two," Rose replied. "Now you have broken the spell of the wild water, I can cross it without harm."

Rose kissed Lily. Lily kissed Rose. Home went Lily. On went Rose.

Now that the spell was broken, Rose swam the wild water without harm. On the far shore she went a short way, she went a long way, and in every footprint grew a small red rose the size of a little-finger ring.

She came to a butterfly caught in a spider's web. She set it free, and on she went.

She went a short way, she went a long way, and she came to a lizard trapped in a clay snare. She set it free, and on she went.

She went a short way, she went a long way, and she came to a flaming hollow. There was no way over it. There was no way under it.

"What does it matter?" said Rose. "I can run."

But as soon as she blew the flames apart, she vanished in a puff of smoke.

At that very moment, in the garden at home, Rose's rose tree wilted again.

"*Now* where has Rose got to?" said Lily.

Off she sped to find her, over the green meadows, past the stream, past the mill, to the shore of the wild water.

Lily lifted her arms and called aloud:

> "Wind, wind, warm and mild,
> Carry me over the water wild,
> To find Rose."

The wind came. The wind lifted her. The wind carried her above the wild water and placed her down gently on the other side.

She went a short way, she went a long way, following Rose's footprints. They led her right to the edge of the flaming hollow, in every footprint a small red rose the size of a little-finger ring.

The sun was going down. Lily lifted her arms and called aloud:

> "All creatures, bird or beast,
> The greatest creature, or the least,
> To whom my sister has been kind,
> Help me, now, Rose to find."

The lizard came. The butterfly came, looping the loop.

"I will find her," said the butterfly.

It fluttered above the flaming hollow, listening to the secrets in the crackling of the flames. Soon it flew back.

"I have found her," it said. "She is a red stone among the other red stones that pave the flaming hollow; but out of her grows a small red rose the size of a little-finger ring."

"I will find her," said the lizard, who was a fire lizard, a salamander.

Into the fire it darted. Out of the fire it darted. It laid a red stone and a small red rose at Lily's feet. As soon as they touched the grass, they vanished in a puff of smoke, and there on that spot stood Rose.

"Come home with me, Rose," begged Lily.

"I have braved two dangers; I can brave three," Rose replied. "Now you have broken the spell of the flaming hollow, I can cross it without harm."

Rose kissed Lily. Lily kissed Rose. Home went Lily. On went Rose.

Now that the spell was broken, Rose ran through the flames without harm. On the far side, she went a short way, she went a long way, and in every footprint grew a small red rose the size of a little-finger ring.

She came to a hummingbird caught in a bird net. She set it free, and on she went.

She went a short way, she went a long way, and she came to a bumblebee caught in a treacle trap. She set it free, and on she went.

She went a short way, she went a long way, and she came to a field mouse caught in a box trap. She set it free, and on she went.

She went a short way, she went a long way, and she came to the witch-queen's rock garden. If there was one acre of it, there were forty; and every square inch of those forty acres was a bare black stone.

The witch-queen was sitting in the middle of it. She was a sight to make young blood run cold. Her teeth were as long as your fingers, her nails were as long and yellow as a kite's claw, and she could crack a nut between her nose and her chin.

She had been spinning, and she had fallen asleep with her spindle on her lap. Her left hand hung down by her side and on her middle finger (for it was too big for any other) gleamed and glowed and glittered the king's little-finger ring.

Rose crept close on tiptoe and began gently to pull the ring off the witch-queen's finger. But the finger cried out:

"Witch-queen, wake,
For my gold ring's sake!"

The witch-queen woke. At the sight of Rose she showed her long teeth in wicked glee and rapped her knuckles with her spindle. Rose vanished in a puff of smoke, and a new black stone fell with a clang and a clatter amid those forty acres of old ones.

The witch-queen sat and stared at the new black stone with wicked eyes. Soon, out of it grew a small red rose the size of a little-finger ring. The witch-queen tore it off.

A second rose grew in its place. The witch-queen tore off the second one. A third rose grew.

The witch-queen thought, and left the third rose. She waved her spindle and out of every bare black stone in those forty acres of rock garden grew a small red rose the size of a little-finger ring.

"Puzzle find the true one," chortled the witch-queen, and she stood up like a tall black bat and stalked into her tall black castle for supper.

At that very moment, in the garden at home, Rose's rose tree wilted a third time.

"*Now* where has Rose got to?" said Lily.

Off she set to find her, over the green meadows, past the stream and past the mill. The wind lifted her over the wild water.

She went a short way, she went a long way, and she came to the flaming hollow. She lifted her arms and called aloud:

"Wind, Wind, swift as a swallow,
Carry me over the flaming hollow,
Rose to follow."

The wind came. The wind lifted her. The wind carried her above the flaming hollow and set her down gently on the other side.

She went a short way, she went a long way, following Rose's footprints. They led her to the witch-queen's rock garden. Out of every stone in that forty acres grew a small red rose the size of a little-finger ring.

The sun was setting. Lily lifted her arms and called aloud:

"All creatures, bird or beast,
The greatest creature, or the least,
To whom my sister has been kind,
Help me, now, Rose to find."

The field mouse came scuttling. The hummingbird came humming. The bumblebee came bumbling.

"I will find her," said the bumblebee.

It preened its wings with its front legs, then away it flew. It bumbled from black stone to black stone, from small red rose to small red rose, all over all those forty acres of rock garden. Soon it bumbled back.

"I have found her," it buzzed. "Only one red rose in all these forty acres has scent and nectar in it."

She led Lily to the true red rose. Lily lifted the stone. It vanished in a puff of smoke, and there stood Rose.

"Wait for me, Lily," she said. "I have braved three dangers; I can brave four. I am going into the castle for the ring while the witch-queen sleeps tonight. Her finger will not wake her again, now that the spell is broken."

"Wait for a moment, Rose," hummed the hummingbird.

The hummingbird flew into the castle and listened to the secrets of the humming, strumming, weaving, heaving thoughts in the witch-queen's mind. Soon it flew back.

"The witch-queen is just off to bed," it told them. "She is going to keep the king's ring under her tongue while she sleeps. She has put a spell on the castle gateway, on each step of the spiral staircase, and on the door-stone of her chamber, so that they will all cry out and wake her if Rose tries to enter."

"Rustling cornstalks!" squeaked the field mouse. "Does she think that is the *only* way into her castle? Stay here, Rose. I will scamper up the ivy and get you the ring myself. Come with me, hummingbird, to bring it back, for the witch-queen has no power over anything in the air."

By now night had fallen, and the moon was coming up. The witch-queen's castle stood gaunt and black against the silver sky, with only the flicker of a candle to mark the witch-queen's chamber.

The field mouse scampered across the forty acres of rock garden to the steep stone wall of the castle, the hummingbird flying behind. The field mouse scampered up the ivy to the narrow window of the witch-queen's chamber, and the hummingbird folded its small wings and sat on the window ledge.

The window was a tight fit even for a field mouse and a hummingbird to squeeze through, but they tucked in their waists and made themselves thin, and they just managed it.

They could hear the witch-queen snoring and snorting in her sleep.

"Bristling barley beards!" squeaked the field mouse. "That ring is choking her!"

The field mouse ran lightly down the wall hangings to the floor, and as lightly up the bed hangings to the pillow. With the tip of its tail it tickled the witch-queen's nose.

"*Atishoo!*" she sneezed in her sleep, with a sound like ripping sackcloth. The ring flew out of her mouth with the sneeze. The hummingbird caught it in midair and out through the slit it slipped and flew, across the forty acres of nectarless roses to Rose. The hummingbird placed the ring on her thumb.

Then Lily lifted her arms and called softly:

> "Wind, Wind, turn around.
> Bear us home to happier ground.
> The ring is found!"

While the witch-queen was still groping blindly in her blankets for the ring, the wind came and lifted Rose and Lily, and carried them back in the moonlight, a short way, a long way, over the flaming hollow, over the wild water, past the mill, past the stream, over the sleeping meadows, and set them down safely at the gate of their own king's castle.

The king was napping in the sickroom when Rose and Lily were brought in to him.

"Why, bless my soul, what's this?" he cried, as Rose laid the ring in his hand.

He slipped it on his little finger, and the instant it snuggled down where it belonged, the two sick princes sat up in their beds, as strong as horses and as right as rain. They stared at Rose and Lily as if they had seen two angels straight from heaven, and Rose and Lily stared back as if they thought the same.

"You had better get up, my boys," said the king, "and we will have a double wedding!"

And they both got up in a flash.

10. The Terrible Tanterabogus

Princess Lunette could not bear the sight of the prince whom her father had said she must marry.

"If he had claws and horns and tusks and a snout and a tail," she wailed, "he would not be any uglier, and I will *not* marry him."

"Lock her in her room till she takes that back," the king told her old nurse, "and give her only dry bread and water."

"Take care the Terrible Tanterabogus doesn't get you," the old nurse warned the weeping princess as she dragged her out of the angry king's presence.

The Terrible Tanterabogus was the bogeyman who, in that country, ate bad children.

"I am not a child any more, afraid of that old bogeyman," muttered Lunette, pushing out her lower lip and wiping her eyes on her long golden hair.

But in fact, she *was* still afraid of him.

All the rest of that day she was locked in her room, and fed only dry bread and water. That night her old nurse slept in the room, with her bed across the door and the key safe under her pillow.

"Trouble is always to be had for the asking," sighed Lunette. "*Now* what shall I do? If I stay and give in, that ugly prince will get me. If I stay and *don't* give in, the Terrible Tanterabogus will get me. I had better not stay at all."

There were pots of poppy plants growing in her room, covered with red and white poppies. Next day, when she was locked in alone, Lunette squeezed the juice out of some of them into a small crystal flask. At dusk, when the old nurse came in with her own supper and Lunette's bread and water, Lunette cried out, "Oh, look, Nurse! A bat at the window!"

The old nurse couldn't stand bats any more than Lunette could stand the ugly prince, so she stumped away to the window to close it with a bang. And while her back was turned, Lunette tipped the poppy juice into her soup.

Now poppy juice makes you sleep – and *how* that old nurse slept that night!

She slept while Lunette put on her jewelled sandals with soles of cork that made her footsteps as silent as a cat's.

She slept while Lunette tied the money she was given to throw among the people when she rode out in the city tightly in a scarf.

She slept while Lunette pulled the key from under her pillow, crawled under her bed to the door, unlocked it, slipped through, locked it again from outside, and dropped the key into a pot of lilies in the palace corridor.

She slept while Lunette dressed herself in a green hunting tunic and leggings from the pages' wardrobe, and twisted up her long golden hair under a page's green cap with a feather to match.

And still the old nurse slept while Lunette stole like a cat down the spiral staircase, wriggled through an open grille in the venison chamber, dropped lightly onto the outside grass, and set out on her journey into the wide world.

Away loped Lunette on her soles of cork, as silent as a shadow in the moonlight, till she came to a poor man's hut on the bank of a river. Below it, on the water, was his boat, moored to a tree.

"Mine be yours, yours be mine!" murmured Lunette at the sleeping man's window.

She laid the scarf filled with money on the poor man's doorstep, scrambled into his boat and untied the rope. The current was swift and strong and, like an arrow loosed from a bow, away sped the boat down the river.

Far she went, far, and far farther than far. The moon went in and there crouched Lunette in the darkness, longing for daybreak, and telling herself, "Trouble is always to be had for the asking. *Now* what shall I do? The river has got me now. But rather the river than that awful prince or the Terrible Tanterabogus!"

Daybreak came. The river grew wilder, for a thunderstorm had swollen its waters, which now rushed seaward, crested with foam, lifting Lunette's boat high and crashing it into a tangle of tree roots under the bank. As it rocked there, Lunette saw a small furry creature washed out of the crumbling bank, saw two tiny paws lifted like praying hands out of the spray, and heard a faint, plaintive cry for help.

"Mine be yours, yours be mine!" called Lunette to the river.

She kicked off her left jewelled sandal in exchange for the struggling little creature; the river seized the sandal and whirled it away, bobbing like a toy cork boat. She threw out the rope that had moored her own boat as a lifeline, and pulled it back in with a half-drowned mole clinging limply to it.

"King Moldiwarp thanks you straight from his heart," said the mole, bowing, then straightened the tiny gold crown on his tiny sleek head. "Shall we step onto dry land while we can?"

Lunette moored the boat to a tree root. Across the writhing roots they scrambled ashore.

"Madam," said King Moldiwarp (for you can't bamboozle a mole with a page's tunic and leggings), "all the moles in my kingdom are at your service. If ever you need help, think of me, and I will be with you."

So, exchanging courtly bows, they parted.

Lunette stumbled on through a wood, left foot shoeless, till she came to a hollow tree with bees flying in and out of it. From within the tree came the saddest bee-music she had ever heard. She asked a worker bee who was landing with its load, "Why do you all sing so sadly?"

"When our hearts are sad, why shouldn't our song be sad?" the bee replied. "We are sad because we're losing our eggs as fast as our queen can lay them. Every day, along comes a bear who puts in its paw and breaks off a chunk of honeycomb to eat, and cells full of young bees with it."

"I can stop the bear from doing that," Lunette told the bee.

She got damp clay and filled in the hole in the tree till it was a slit just big enough for bees to pass in and out, but too small for a bear's paw to go through. As it grew dry and hard, out flew the roly-poly queen, her five eyes popping with joy below her tiny gold crown.

"Madam," she said (for you can't bamboozle a bee with a page's tunic and leggings), "Queen Melissa thanks you straight from her heart. All the bees in my kingdom are at your service. If ever you need help, think of me, and I will be with you."

So, exchanging courtly bows, they parted.

Lunette limped on, left foot shoeless, till, when the sun was high, she came out of the wood, and saw before her a ruined temple in a shady garden. By now she was hungry and thirsty as well as tired, so, sitting down in the shadow of the temple, she ate and ate the juicy berries growing there. Then, leaning against a tree trunk, she fell fast asleep.

Now Lunette was in a kingdom ruled over by a young king. The royal city of that kingdom was not far away, and it was filled with weeping and wailing. Early that morning, a messenger had ridden in, swaying in his saddle with tiredness.

"Sirs," he said to the king's counsellors, all aged men with long white beards, "we have lost the battle and King Zygmund has been taken prisoner. Our enemies have captured the fortress guarding the river mouth, and tomorrow they will ride to capture this city as well."

The old men plucked at their long white beards.

"*Now* what shall we do?" they cried. "We must ask the wise oracle." So they sent word and asked the oracle.

This was the answer the oracle sent back:

> "One who sleeps today at noon,
> Right foot shod, and left foot bare,
> Beside the Temple of the Moon,
> From enemies shall free your land,
> And sit upon your king's right hand,
> And with him throne and kingdom share."

Swiftly and gladly then the old men called for horses; swiftly and gladly they rode out to the ruined Temple of the Moon. There, in its shadow, Lunette was wakened by the ring of hoofs and the tinkle of bridle bells, and opened her eyes to see a circle of long white beards around her.

"Never was a stranger so welcome, Sir!" they greeted her (for, not being moles or bees, they *were* bamboozled by the page's tunic and leggings). "By what noble name may we address you?"

"I must tell them a fierce one," thought Lunette, "so that they will never guess I am a runaway princess in disguise."

So, making her voice as manly and gruff as she could, she said, "The Terrible Tanterabogus."

The whitebeards brushed the ground as they bowed, because the name impressed them tremendously.

"And from where has Lord Terrible Tanterabogus come to us?" they asked.

"From far, and far, and far farther than far," replied the Terrible Tanterabogus.

They gave her a horse (to her great comfort), and rode with joy back to the royal palace. And there they told her what the wise oracle had told them.

Lunette's heart sank with a bump. But she managed to reply, in her Tanterabogus voice, "Leave me alone now, my lords, to consider my strategy."

Joyfully they bowed and withdrew.

"Trouble is always to be had for the asking," Lunette moaned. "*Now* what shall I do?"

She thought of Queen Melissa, and at once the roly-poly queen bee was with her, her five eyes popping with interest under her tiny golden crown as Lunette told her story.

"Madam," said Queen Melissa, "get some riding boots made tonight and early tomorrow morning, ride out alone to meet the enemy. Leave all the rest to me."

The royal cordwainers toiled all night to make the Terrible Tanterabogus a pair of riding boots, and early next morning Lunette put them on (slipping her one jewelled sandal into the wide sleeve of her page's tunic) and rode out alone to meet the enemy.

Far across the plain she saw a great army advancing, the morning sunlight glinting on rank beyond rank of burnished helmets and coats of chainmail. Then suddenly she saw the ordered ranks break into wild confusion: horses reared up, riders were thrown and trampled, the mules who pulled the cannons plunged and turned tail, the oxen who pulled the baggage trains went berserk, and the elephants who pulled the battering rams ran amok.

Every bee in the kingdom flew that morning to help Lunette. Swarm after swarm after swarm swooped to attack. The enemy were stung, and stung, and stung again, till at last they wheeled around and fled. They were stung as they galloped across the plain to the shore, and they were stung as they boarded their ships in panic, and in panic put out to sea.

Lunette, sitting on her horse on the cliff top, watched their sails grow small on the skyline. Then she rode quietly back to a city where the people raised the roofs in praise of the Terrible Tanterabogus.

"Sleep now, Lord Terrible Tanterabogus," the whitebeards begged her, "so that tomorrow you can re-capture the fortress our enemies still hold and set King Zygmund free."

Joyfully they bowed and withdrew.

"Trouble is always to be had for the asking," Lunette sighed. "*Now* what shall I do?"

She thought of King Moldiwarp, and at once he was with her in his sleek fur coat, his tiny gold crown tipped over his long nose as he listened to her story.

"Madam," he said, "lead what is left of King Zygmund's army to the fortress tomorrow. Go dressed as a herald, and proclaim the message I will give you. Leave all the rest to me."

Early next morning Lunette rode out, at the head of her

army, to the fortress guarding the river mouth. She wore a herald's tabard over her hunting tunic and a herald's trumpet was slung across her chest.

At the fortress gate she sounded her herald's trumpet, and proclaimed to the warders in her Tanterabogus voice:

"The Terrible Tanterabogus gives you till noon to deliver King Zygmund to him unharmed and to leave the fortress. Already its walls are being undermined. Come to them half an hour before noon, and what you will see will make your hair stand on end."

The warders laughed, but half an hour before noon the walls were so thronged with soldiers that you could not have dropped a stone among them. They looked right, they looked left, they looked up, and they looked down, but they couldn't see anything new but the herald quietly sitting on his horse, and, behind him, the ranks of his army. Jeers broke out.

"You have not lifted a single hair on our heads yet, Terrible Tanterabogus!"

But suddenly across the jeers sounded a voice, shrill with alarm.

"Look! Look! The ground is heaving!"

And now from the whole ring of the city's walls, the same cry rose.

"Look! Look! The ground is heaving!"

Every mole in the kingdom was toiling underground that day to help Lunette. Moles come to the surface at eight, at noon, and at four, King Moldiwarp had told her; each time, the soil would heave for half an hour before they threw up

103

their molehills. Seen from above, that circle of heaving earth was so sinister that the hair of the watchers really did stand on end with terror. The gates were opened, the keys were delivered to the herald, and the captive King Zygmund rode out unharmed. The enemy garrison marched out in haste, boarded their ships and scuttled away.

Lunette's jewelled sandal had been on its own adventure. When Lunette had kicked it off to buy King Moldiwarp's life, its cork sole had kept it afloat as the river whirled it away. A mouse, swept from the bank by a large wave, had been catapulted right into it and was carried by it down the river as far as the river mouth. Here it was caught up in a crosscurrent, which threw it against the wall of the fortress again and again, just beneath the barred grille of a dungeon.

It was in this very dungeon that young King Zygmund had been imprisoned. Peering out, he had been aware of the river rising till now and again a wave washed in at the bars. When he saw the flash of jewels spinning back and forth in the water, he put his hand out between the bars, waited, pounced, and pulled the sandal in.

Out sprang the mouse who sat up on the dungeon floor, wiped his whiskers, folded his paws, and bowed with extreme politeness.

"Sir, my name is Souris," he said. (He was a French mouse.) "Sir, I owe you my life. If, sir, the help of a common house mouse with a taste for travel is ever of any use to you, I am at your service any hour of the day or night."

King Zygmund thanked him gravely, but all the while he could not tear his gaze from the sandal in his hand. It was so delicate and dainty, so foolish yet so brave, that there and then he fell head over heels in love with the delicate, dainty, brave and foolish lady who had worn it.

"Have you travelled far, my friend?" he asked craftily.

"Far, and far, and far farther than far," Souris told him.

"All the way in your jewelled boat?" asked King Zygmund.

"No, sir, only the last lap of my journey," Souris replied. "Dry land gave way under me, but the river offered me this boat, and – *voila*! Pray, sir, how do you yourself come to be here?"

King Zygmund told him.

"Then, sir," said Souris, "I will stay here with you, and run around the fortress, picking you up crumbs of information."

"I have only crumbs of dry bread to offer you in return, my friend," King Zygmund warned him.

"*Zut!* Who cares?" said Souris. "A mouse with a taste for travel is glad of what he gets."

He brushed his whiskers and scuttled away. Soon he was back, his beady eyes gleaming.

"Sir, your whitebeards have found a champion," he announced. "He is the Terrible Tanterabogus, and the wise oracle says he will free you and share your throne and kingdom."

"Who *is* the Terrible Tanterabogus?" King Zygmund asked, astonished at this news.

"Sir, in one land I passed through," Souris told him, "I gathered he is a bogeyman who eats bad children."

"Share my throne with a child-eating bogeyman?" exclaimed King Zygmund, horrified. "My whitebeards must be mad to believe the oracle foretold *that*!"

Next evening, Souris came scampering in, his whiskers bristling with excitement.

"Sir, the Terrible Tanterabogus is outside the fortress with an army, and he says you will be free by noon!"

Just before noon the next day, Souris urged, "Quick, quick, King Zygmund! Let me leap into your sleeve! They are coming to release you!"

A key turned rustily in the lock. King Zygmund was led along dark passages, up stairs in the thickness of the fortress walls, and out into clear daylight. He was given a horse, the gates were opened, and out from his prison he rode free, to meet the Terrible Tanterabogus.

King Zygmund could not imagine anything less like a child-eating bogeyman than the Terrible Tanterabogus.

They rode back to the royal city along roads strewn with flowers, enjoying each other's company. When they sat side by side in the throne room, and the whitebeards and the courtiers withdrew, King Zygmund whispered, "And now, Terrible Tanterabogus, to mark my deep gratitude, I am going to show you my most precious possession!"

And from his left sleeve he pulled out the jewelled sandal.

To his astonishment, the Terrible Tanterabogus snatched it from him, and was away like a hare down the length of the throne room. Away like a hound went King

Zygmund in pursuit, and caught the Terrible Tanterabogus at the door.

"Give me back my sandal, Terrible Tanterabogus," he pleaded. "It means more to me than my life."

"It was mine before it was yours!" cried Lunette, and in her excitement she quite forgot to use her Tanterabogus voice. "Pull off my riding boots, and you shall see!"

She sat on the throne again, and King Zygmund pulled off her riding boots. She slipped her left foot into his sandal, and it fitted like a glove. Then out of her own sleeve she took its partner, and slipped her right foot into that. There could not be the least doubt in the world that these sandals had been made for her.

"But if that is so," thought King Zygmund in despair, "the lady I love doesn't exist!"

Then in his mind's eye he saw again the Terrible Tanterabogus running down the throne room. "The Terrible Tanterabogus runs like a girl," he thought. "And now I come to think of it, he walks like a girl; and, when he forgets, he talks like a girl; he has a girl's small feet, and a girl's small waist. My eyes and my ears and my heart all tell me he is a girl."

He shook his right sleeve, and out sprang Souris, scampering around the room, scratching and scrabbling the floor with his feet so that the Terrible Tanterabogus would hear him.

The Terrible Tanterabogus heard him. The Terrible Tanterabogus saw him. The Terrible Tanterabogus gave a shriek that rang all round the throne room, all round the palace, all round the city. It was the high-pitched shriek of a girl.

As she jumped away from the mouse, Lunette's page's cap fell off her head, and her knee-long golden hair came tumbling down.

"O Terrible Tanterabogus, will you marry me," asked King Zygmund, laughing, "and really share my throne and kingdom?"

"Mine by yours, yours be mine," smiled Lunette. And she didn't have to marry the ugly prince, after all.

11. Cocorico and Coquelicot

The farm roosters were crowing the world awake when the farmer's son was born, so they called him Cocorico (which means *cock-a-doodle-doo* in French).

Cocorico could crow before he could talk. He could strut before he could walk. Even his hair stuck up like feathers. And from the moment he could crawl, he went out every morning before breakfast to pass the time of day with Roo, the farmyard's chief rooster.

Roosters are knowing birds because they get up so early. And Roo was wiser than most, for he was older than most. Because he was Cocorico's special friend, his life was spared till he was too tough for the pot; and after that, he just went on living and living because he was too tough to die.

So Roo gave Cocorico many tips about the weather and the farm, and Cocorico passed them all on to his father. Over the years, the farmer never once found his son to be wrong. If Cocorico said today would be a good day for winnowing or a bad day for ploughing, however unlikely it seemed, a high wind or storms of rain always blew up later.

Early one January, when Cocorico had just grown up, Roo told him, "There will be no barley harvest this year, dear boy."

"Why not, dear Roo?" asked Cocorico.

"It is the flame that falls into the seed that makes the barley grow, dear boy," said Roo. "It only falls in the twelve days after Christmas, and this year it hasn't fallen. It will not fall again till men get busy and renew it."

When Cocorico went indoors to breakfast, he told his father, "Father, you will eat no bite of any barley you sow this spring. You will get more good from it if you leave it stored in the grain loft."

Because Cocorico had never been wrong, the farmer sowed no barley that spring. But because he was afraid of being laughed at, he didn't tell anybody why. When harvest time came round, there was not a handful of barley to be reaped in the whole kingdom. Every grain loft in the land was empty except for that of Cocorico's father.

The king heard about this and he sent for the farmer.

"Tell me," said the king, "why is your grain loft still full when all the others are as bare as my hand?"

"Your Majesty," said the farmer, "because I stored my grain this spring instead of sowing it."

"Tell me, why did you do that?" asked the king.

"Your Majesty," said the farmer, "because my son told me to."

"Send for your son," said the king.

When Cocorico came, the king said, "Tell me, why did you tell your father not to sow his grain this spring?"

"Your Majesty," said Cocorico, "because I knew it wouldn't grow."

"Tell me, why not?" asked the king.

"Your Majesty," said Cocorico, "because no flame fell into the seed in the twelve days after Christmas."

The king nodded his head. He knew about seed flame needing to fall. It is a king's business to know such things.

"Tell me, will it fall next year?" he asked.

"Your Majesty," said Cocorico, "only if men get busy and renew it."

Now the king was very old, and he had no child to rule after him. For a long time he had been seeking for someone to be his heir, someone who would care for the kingdom as a king should.

"I tell you," he said now, "I think you may be just the young man I am looking for. Go and get this seed flame renewed, and you shall be heir to my kingdom."

Cocorico went back to the farmyard, and told all this to Roo.

"It will not be easy, but it will not be hard," Roo told him. "The flame comes from Out of This World. All you have to do, dear boy, is to marry a princess from Out of This World, and she will bring back the flame as her wedding gift."

"Where is Out of This World, dear Roo?" asked Cocorico.

"Out of this world, of course, dear boy," said Roo. "You simply go north till you get there. Ask the cockerel of the north when you can go no further."

So Cocorico set out on his journey to Out of This World. North he walked, and north he walked, and still north he walked, till his shoes were in holes, and his socks, too. He walked for months and months; he walked till nearly Christmas.

All the time it got colder and colder, till at last he came to a land where there was nothing but snow on all four sides of him, and the snow in front of him rose like a wall. And there he met the cockerel of the north.

"Am I near to Out of This World, dear cockerel?" he asked.

"There is only this wall between you, dear boy," the cockerel of the north replied after a moment, flapping his wings to keep warm. "This is the place where, once every twenty-four hours, the earth turns on its hinges. Wait till you hear them creak, and you can slip through."

Cocorico waited till the earth turned on its hinges. He heard them creak and he slipped through, and then he was in Out of This World.

Out of This World was indeed out of this world. He slipped through from grey skies to blue, from snowfields to cornfields standing tall and golden, from winds as sharp as a shearing-knife to air as soft as a May morning.

He came to a well, brimming with bright water, and he lay down and drank from it. The water of that well was sweeter than home-made lemonade. As he drank, he heard a girl's voice singing, and it seemed to be coming nearer. In a flash

Cocorico was on his feet and hidden among the foliage of the tree overhanging the well.

From within his screen of leaves Cocorico saw a pair of bare feet pause under the tree, and a plain white robe above them. Then he saw the white-clad shoulders and the tied-back blonde hair of a girl as she knelt at the edge of the well, her hand on a water jar. Before she dipped it, she leaned forward and stared at herself in the calm mirror of the water.

Cocorico bent down from among the branches to stare at her, too. The face he saw in the well was fresh and young and sparkling, with a red poppy behind one ear and a beauty spot near the left corner of her mouth. He thought it was the most charming face he had ever seen.

Then, all at once, the smiling eyes widened and the girl's whole body froze. Close to her dazzling reflection Cocorico saw what she had just seen – his own reflection.

Dark-haired boy and fair-haired girl stared at each other in the water without speaking. Then he saw her reflection place a finger on its lips. A moment later, the mirror was shattered into ripples as she dipped her water jar and stood up, lifting it to her shoulder.

As she slowly moved away, she started to sing again, softly yet clearly, as if her song was meant for him. And this was what she sang:

> "If Coquelicot you would win,
> Rooster must not crow,
> And horn must not blow.
> Open the gate, and enter in.

113

If you seek flame to light your seeds,
Do not forget
That never yet
Has holly lost its glossy leaves.

When twenty golden girls you see,
All charm and grace,
All fair of face,
Remember me! Remember me!"

Cocorico waited till the song had died away and then he slid down the tree trunk. He smoothed his hair that stuck up like feathers with water from the well, washed his hands and face and pulled up his stockings that were full of holes. Then, taking a deep breath, he followed the path from the well.

It wandered up a slope of laden peach and pear trees towards a huge patterned golden gate, through which he could see, in silhouette, a hanging horn, and a guard lazily tossing dice as he leaned against it. Beyond rose a stately hall, with walls of silver under a roof of gold.

As Cocorico came nearer, he saw beside the path a golden rooster on a tall lookout post. He thought it was a golden weathervane until, as he came out from the shelter of the fruit trees, it flapped its wings and stretched its neck, and stood on its toes to crow.

"Psst, dear rooster!" Cocorico called softly in cockerel language. "I am Cocorico – don't crow for *me*! Help me instead to stop that horn from blowing."

The golden rooster eyed him shrewdly, then flew over the golden gate, pounced on the guard's dice as they were in midair, and flapped away. The guard dashed after it, cursing as he ran. Cocorico thrust his hand through the gate's golden metalwork, lifted the bar, opened the gate, and walked in.

He took the horn, in case the warder came back and blew it, and then he walked up to the glittering hall and went inside.

It was empty except for a large king, asleep on his throne, his crown on the back of his head. As Cocorico strode up the hall with ringing footsteps, the king woke up and yawned a mighty yawn. Then his gaze fell on Cocorico, and he stared and rubbed his eyes.

"I suppose you have come for one of my daughters, dear boy?" he rumbled.

"Yes, please, Your Majesty," said Cocorico.

"Well, dear boy," said the king, "the rooster didn't crow and the horn didn't blow, so you're over the first of your hurdles. Now tell me this: will you look after her for as long as there are leaves on trees, or for as long as not?"

"As long as not will be winter, when the seed flame falls," thought Cocorico. "Is that the right answer?"

Then he remembered the song of the girl at the well, and instead he answered, "For as long as there *are* leaves on trees, please, Your Majesty."

"Oh, dear boy!" exclaimed the king in surprise. "You'll only look after her in summer, then?"

"All the year round, please, Your Majesty," said Cocorico:

115

"Do not forget
That never yet
Has holly lost its glossy leaves."

"Aha!" chuckled the king, rubbing his hands, well pleased. "Two hurdles over! Now, *which* daughter, dear boy? It's no use saying you don't mind. You *must* name the one you want."

Again Cocorico remembered the song at the well.

"Coquelicot, please, Your Majesty," he said.

"Coquelicot, eh?" chuckled the king. "Well, dear boy, if you can pick her out, you're welcome to her. That's your fourth hurdle, and your last."

Taking the horn from Cocorico's hand, he blew a loud blast on it. At once the staircase from the rooms above was alive with footsteps and voices. Then in trooped the princesses, four, eight, ten, twenty of them. They made a ring round Cocorico, took hands, and invited him archly:

"Choose, dear boy!"

Cocorico ran his fingers through his hair, making it stick up like feathers more than ever. For those twenty princesses were as much alike as a ring of fence stakes (though much more beautiful, of course). And every one of them, he could have sworn, was the girl he had seen at the well.

He looked at them all again. Each had the same glowing face, the same sparkling glance, the same blonde locks, the same grace; each gleamed in a long golden dress; each wore a golden star in her golden crown. There simply wasn't a hair to choose between them.

And then, he remembered something! He walked around

the ring of laughing, golden girls again, and stopped in front of the one with a beauty spot near the left corner of her mouth. He leaned forward, and kissed those lips. And all Coquelicot's sisters clapped their hands and cried:

"Right, dear boy!"

On Christmas Day, Cocorico and his bride Coquelicot said farewell to the king and her nineteen charming sisters. This time Cocorico didn't wear holes in his wedding shoes, nor his wedding socks, either, for the king sent a strong north wind to carry them swiftly home.

And for all the twelve nights after Christmas, Coquelicot's dowry of seed flames fell thick over all the kingdom. There had never been such a barley harvest as the one that followed, even in Roo's long memory.

As soon as the harvest was safe in the kingdom's grain lofts, the old king made Cocorico his heir and in due course he and Coquelicot became king and queen of the land.

Roo helped them to rule it well with his store of farmyard wisdom. In fact, a tough old bird like Roo is probably still helping them.

12. The Mirror on the Mountain

When the King of Spain's daughter was sixteen years old, her old chaperone went to the king.

"Sire, the Infanta is growing up fast," she said. (Infanta is the Spanish word for a princess.) "Remember, it is her fate that she will marry a young man who brings her to you, from a mirror on a mountain." "Bless me, is she as old as that already?" exclaimed the king. "Let me put on my thinking cap." And he sent for it from his treasury.

"I shall have my men find me a mountain," he announced, when the thinking cap was on, "one mile high, one mile wide and one mile long. On its peak they shall build me a crystal castle with ramparts that cannot be climbed. I will place a guard at every nook, and two at every cranny. I will turn a river into a moat. If anyone can bring the Infanta to me from *that* mirror, he *deserves* to marry her!"

It was no sooner said than done. In no time at all, the mountain was found, the river was turned into a moat, the castle was built, and the Infanta Esperanta Esterella Isabella was sitting beside the fountain in its rose garden with her chaperone.

Now just over the border, in Portugal, lived a poor widow with her son, Torto, and her stepson, Benito. Torto was the apple of her eye, but Benito was the dust beneath her feet.

Who had to get up in the dark, light the fire, and fetch water from the spring? Benito.

And who, as the sun rose one morning, saw the flashing of a fiery mirror on a distant mountain top? Benito.

He rushed indoors, his buckets of water spilling over.

"Stepmother," he said, "please give me food for a journey. I have seen a mirror on a mountain, and I feel I have to go to it."

His stepmother ran to the spring, to see the mirror with her own eyes. She ran back home and pulled Torto out of his snug bed.

"Get up, lazybones!" she scolded. "Run to the spring and look at the mirror on the mountain. That is where your fortune lies. Go now and find it, or Benito will find it first."

She got out her husband's best festival coat for Torto to wear. She filled a backpack with cake for Torto to eat on the way. And she put in a bottle of good red wine from Oporto for when Torto was thirsty.

"Go on then," she cried, pushing him out of the door, "and put your best foot forward!"

For the rest of the morning, the stepmother kept Benito busy. She found task after task for him to do. But when she could find no more tasks, he finally set out in his dirty old coat with holes in the elbows, only a dry crust of bread in his backpack, and an empty bottle which he filled with water from the spring as he went by.

Torto walked along grandly in his father's fine coat.

"All I need now," he said to himself, "is a feather in my cap."

He saw a magpie sitting in a tree, half black as night, half white as day. Torto lifted a stone into his hand and threw it at the bird. *Squawk* went the magpie, and a black feather fell from her tail as she flew away.

Torto put the feather in his cap, and went whistling on his way. He met nobody till he came to a little old man sitting under an old thorn bush. His head was as bald as a basin, and he wore a leather apron and crooked spectacles on his nose. He was sewing fine snakeskin shoes.

"Sewing leather is hungry work," the little man greeted Torto. "Could a fine young man in a festival coat spare an old shoemaker a crust of bread?"

"No," said Torto curtly. "I have only cake." And he walked on with his head in the air.

Again Torto met nobody till he came to a little old man sitting on a grassy slope. He wore a jaunty hat and had silver buckles on his shoes. His cloak flapped in the wind as he strummed on a harp, singing over and over again:

"The sun, the moon, the stars are bright."

"Singing is thirsty work," the little man greeted Torto. "Could a fine young man in a festival coat spare an old harper a drink of water?"

"No," said Torto curtly. "I have only wine." And he walked on with his head in the air.

When the sun was overhead he came to a wide river. On the other side was a mountain, a mile wide, a mile long, a mile high, and he could see a crystal castle, perched on its topmost crag. Torto racked his brains, but he couldn't think of a way of reaching it.

He sat down under a tree on the riverbank. He ate up all his cake. He drank up all his wine.

"Well, there is the mirror on the mountain," he said to himself. "But I've no idea how to reach it, not one. I may as well have my siesta here, and then go home again."

He stretched himself out in the shade of the tree and, in two flicks of a cow's tail, he was fast asleep.

Benito stood up from filling his bottle at the spring. Overhead, a magpie began to chatter. "Here's a feather to put in your cap, my boy, a feather to put in your cap."

And she let one of her white wing feathers flutter to his feet.

Benito nodded his thanks to the magpie, and placed the feather in his cap. "A thousand thanks, señorita," he called to her politely, then went whistling on his way.

He met nobody till he came to the little bald shoemaker sewing fine snakeskin shoes under his old thorn bush.

"Sewing leather is hungry work," the little man greeted him. "Is that a crust I hear rattling in your backpack?"

"It is," replied Benito, "and you can have half of it."

He sat down beside the old shoemaker and they munched Benito's crust together.

"Those are fine shoes you are making," said Benito.

"A finer point to my needle," said the old shoemaker, "would make them finer still."

"Let me see it," said Benito.

He ground the blunt point on a rough stone. Before he could say *hey presto*! the needle was as sharp as a needle. And before he could say it again, the snakeskin shoes were finished.

"The one who sharpens the needle gets the shoes," said the old shoemaker, slipping them into Benito's knapsack.

"But they are far too fine to walk in," said Benito, thanking him.

"They are not meant to walk in," the old man replied, twinkling over the top of his spectacles. "You will find out what they are for when the time comes."

Benito went on. Again he met nobody till he came to the little old harper sitting on his green slope, his silver buckles glinting in the sun, his cloak flapping in the wind as he strummed his harp and sang over and over again:

"The sun, the moon, the stars are bright."

"Singing is thirsty work," the little man greeted him. "Is that a bottle of water I hear rolling in your backpack?"

"It is," replied Benito, "and you can have half of it."

He sat down beside the old harper and they drank Benito's bottle of water together.

"That was a fine song you were singing," said Benito.

"If one of my strings was not broken," said the old harper, "it would be a finer song still."

"Let me see it," said Benito.

He took the white magpie feather from his cap, twirled it into a string, and stretched it over the gap. The harper drew his hand across the strings, and the white feather sang with the rest:

> "The sun, the moon, the stars are bright;
> But brighter still shines forth earth's light."

"The one who mends the harpstring gets the harp," said the old harper, slipping it into Benito's knapsack.

"But I don't know how to play a harp," said Benito, thanking him.

"You will," the old man replied, eyes and shoe buckles twinkling, "when you have no idea, not one."

Benito went on till he came to a wide river. He stood on its bank, beside the tree beneath which Torto was sleeping. But he didn't see Torto, because he was staring ahead. On the other side was a mountain, a mile wide, a mile long, a mile high. He could see a castle of crystal perched on its topmost crag. He racked his brains, but he couldn't think of a way of reaching it.

"Well, there is my mirror on its mountain," he said to

himself. "But I have no idea how to reach it, not one. Didn't the old harper say that was the time to play the harp?"

He took out the harp and twanged its white feather string. The harpstring sang:

> "He who weds is he who woos.
> If to be a prince you choose,
> Boy, you have no time to lose.
> Quick, put on your snakeskin shoes!"

Quickly Benito kicked off his old clumsy peasant shoes with holes in the soles and quickly he slid his feet into the fine, elegant, supple snakeskin ones.

At once he found himself lifted into the air and wafted over the river. He flew as birds fly in fables, swift and sure in their flight; and if the guards taking their siestas in all the castle's nooks and crannies felt his shadow pass over them, they thought it was only the shadow of a bird.

Light as a bird he landed on the castle's crystal battlements, and looked down into a rose garden in the shelter of their walls. Among the roses, by the cool, glittering fountain, the Infanta Esperanta Esterella Isabella was taking her siesta, and nearby, her chaperone was taking hers. With just one flying leap, Benito stood beside the sleeping princess.

She was a sight for sore eyes – or indeed for any eyes at all. With her long eyelashes, and her long black hair escaping from beneath her lace mantilla, a kind of veil, she looked as beautiful as a princess ever could. Benito felt he could never bear to let her out of his sight again. He stood as still as a stone while he stared, and stared, and stared.

The singing of Benito's harpstring had wakened Torto from his siesta. Lying drowsily beneath his tree, he saw Benito slip on his snakeskin shoes, saw him soar like a bird across the river and up the mountain, skimming the treetops and getting smaller and smaller till he was a black speck on the crystal battlements.

"Ah-ha!" said Torto to himself. "What one can do, two can do."

He ran softly back to the green slope, where the old harper still sat, his cloak flapping in the wind, his silver buckles glinting in the sun. He was strumming a new harp and still was singing over and over again:

"The sun, the moon, the stars are bright."

Torto crept up silently behind him. He knocked the old harper's jaunty hat over his eyes, snatched the harp, and disappeared among the trees. He ran softly on to the old thorn bush, where the little old shoemaker still sat, stitching busily now at a pair of bat-skin shoes.

When they were done, he put them on the grass beside him while he yawned, took off his spectacles and carefully rubbed them with a scrap of chamois leather. When he turned to pick up the shoes again, they had vanished into thin air.

Already by then the bat-skin shoes were on Torto's feet. But his feet still stood firm on the ground. Torto plucked at the harp, but it made no sound. Then he noticed the gap in the strings and saw again, in his mind's eye, Benito twanging a twisted white feather; so he took the black feather from his own cap, and twirled it into a harpstring.

As soon as he twanged this harpstring, it began to sing:

> "He who weds is he who woos.
> If to be a prince you choose,
> Boy, you have no time to lose.
> Follow, follow, bat-skin shoes!"

At once Torto found himself lifted into the air and wafted over the river. He flew as birds fly in fables, swift and sure in their flight; and if the guards still taking their siestas in all the castle's nooks and crannies felt his shadow pass over them, they thought it was only the shadow of a bird.

Light as a bird he landed on the castle's crystal battlements, and looked down into the rose garden. There he saw the Infanta Esperanta Esterella Isabella taking her siesta by the fountain; and there he saw Benito standing as still as a stone beside her while he stared, and stared, and stared.

The Infanta was not really still taking her siesta. The breeze of Benito's coming had awakened her, but she lay still as if asleep and peeped at him through her lashes, to see what he was like, this stranger she was to marry.

She did not mind that he looked poor and had holes in the elbows of his coat. She looked past all that at his kind eyes, and she hugged herself with joy. For the longer she looked at Benito, the more she saw in him to love.

When she opened her eyes and smiled at him, he thought she was as marvellous as a magpie, her hair so black, her skin so white, and her eyes both black and white.

"I am glad it is you," she told him, "who will take me to my father."

She spoke in a whisper, but her chaperone was trained to hear whispers even in her sleep. She woke up and all *she* saw was a peasant boy in rags. *This* was not the bridegroom she had dreamed of for the Infanta!

The scream she gave startled all the guards out of their siestas. Out they rushed, one from every nook, two from every cranny, shouting as they clattered up the crystal stairways.

And as they poured into the rose garden, Torto took a flying leap from the battlements and scooped up the Infanta. Away went bat-skin shoes, away went Torto in them, away went the Infanta flung across his shoulder, flying as birds fly in fables, swift and sure between the clouds and the treetops.

If Benito had stared too long before, he did not do so now. Away after them went snakeskin shoes, away went Benito in them, flying as birds fly in fables, swift and sure between the treetops and the clouds.

On they all flew to the north until, as the sun went down in the sky, they left the coast of Spain behind them and began

127

to fly over water. Still they flew north until, as the full moon came up, they flew over another coast, and misty land lay below them.

"What country is this?" Torto wondered to himself.

But the Infanta, who (being a princess) had studied her maps, knew it must be Ireland.

Below them they could see lights whirling in rings and spirals. Along the margins of the bogs, the will-o'-the-wisps were dancing with feet as light as eggshells. When they saw Torto flying, black against the moon, the will-o'-the-wisps called out:

> "Moon and mist and marsh together
> Make the merriest dancing weather.
> Flying shoes of bat-skin leather,
> Dance with us among the heather!"

The call drew the bat-skin shoes down to earth, and Torto in them, and with Torto the Infanta, flung like a sack over his shoulder. Seeing Benito now black against the moon, the will-o'-the-wisps called again:

> "Moon and mist and marsh together
> Make the merriest dancing weather.
> Flying shoes of snakeskin leather,
> Dance with us among the heather!"

Now will-o'-the-wisps have flighty memories, as giddy as their changeable bodies, and they forgot that ever since

St Patrick turned all the snakes out of Ireland, no part of a snake can land on Irish soil. So their call failed to draw the snakeskin shoes, and Benito in them, down to earth.

Torto was not so lucky. A thousand small will-o'-the-wisp hands held him down, and he loosened his grip on the Infanta.

As Benito passed overhead, he swooped; he held out his arms to the Infanta, she held out hers to him, and he caught her. Away to the south they flew together in the moonlight, in each other's arms, till they came at sunrise to the King of Spain's own palace, and a joyful welcome home.

Meanwhile, Torto was still in Ireland.

"Dance with us! Dance with us, Torto!" cried the will-o'-the-wisps.

So, helter-skelter, Torto danced with them. They leaped around him like bright spots of quicksilver, but Torto was angry and danced like a lump of lead.

"Strip off his bat-skin shoes!" the will-o'-the-wisps shrieked, enraged – and a thousand small hands did so.

"Since you cannot dance," said the will-o'-the-wisps, "make music for *us* to dance to."

So, helter-skelter, Torto played his harp. As he sullenly twanged his black feather string, it sang:

> "The sun, the moon, the stars are bright;
> But earth remains as black as night."

"He is playing lies!" cried the will-o'-the-wisps. "Take his harp away, and cast him in the bog!"

And it was in the bog that Torto found himself when he woke at dawn, filthy and aching. He scrambled out of it with a face as long as two days put together. Bruised and barefoot, he limped his way to the Irish coast, found a ship heading south, and worked his passage back to Portugal. And so he came home to his mother as poor as he had left her, and with his father's best festival coat caked in Irish mud.

But from that day to this, he has never again thrown a stone at a magpie. So you see, there is still hope for him.

13. The Four-Leaved Clover

Sappho was one of the queen's milkmaids. Outdoors in all weather, breathing sweet air, she was as brown as a peat pool, as strong as a heather root, and as wholesome as the new milk she brought from meadow to castle each sunrise.

The path led her past the head of a valley filled from side to side with a forest of red yew trees. One morning, as she walked by with a pail of milk on her head, she stopped dead in surprise. For, rising above the treetops, she saw spiral stone chimneys where she had never seen chimneys before; and out of the spiral chimneys rose spiral columns of smoke.

"But a house can't spring up overnight, like a mushroom!" Sappho exclaimed.

She lifted the pail from her head as she stood gazing, and the wreath of fresh grass it had rested on slipped from her head and fell to the ground. At once the chimneys vanished, along with the smoke.

Sappho picked up her grass garland. Back came the chimneys, along with the smoke. Puzzled, she sat down and took the wreath apart. And among the meadow flowers and meadow grasses, she found a four-leaved clover.

Now a four-leaved clover, as Sappho knew, can make the right kind of eyes see things other eyes just can't see. Not everybody has the right kind of eyes, but Sappho had them.

She took the four-leaved clover home and planted it in a pot on her window ledge. It put down roots, and grew. And, her tongue being as small as her heart was big, she did not tell a soul what she had seen.

Winter came round. The cows were brought inside to their stalls. Sappho no longer passed the forest of red yew trees every morning.

But every day now she saw Prince Pepin, the king's only son, ride out to hunt. Every day she would watch him ride out of sight, and then sigh, as half her heart had gone with him.

One day Prince Pepin did not come back from hunting, and a letter fell from a swirl of mist into the queen's lap. It demanded the kingdom as the prince's ransom.

"But if, in spite of all my safeguards, you can rescue him," it ended, "you will never again be troubled by Simeon the Sorcerer."

Simeon the Sorcerer was a dreaded name in that kingdom. No one knew him, no one had ever seen him, no one knew where he came from, and no one knew where he lived. But three years ago he had stolen the queen's luck-bringing black bull calf, Star, whom Sappho had brought up by hand; and since then, nothing in castle or cottage had been safe from him.

The king sent out his men to scour the whole kingdom – every city, every hamlet, every hill, every valley, every forest, every plain. But they couldn't find any trace of Simeon the Sorcerer, nor of Prince Pepin.

Sappho watched them go, watched them return.

"Hmm, I wonder..." she said to herself.

Night and snow were falling together as she pinned her four-leaved clover over her heart and set out for the head of the valley. If the chimneys were there, night and the snowstorm blotted them out. She said a small charm, then she said a big charm, and then she plunged into the black, black void of the forest.

Soon she saw gleams of light between the yew trees and before long she stood in front of a vast black mansion, scattered from ground to turrets with lighted arrow-slits. Bursts of wild music came to her, bursts of loud laughter and revelry.

She dimly saw that she was in a great, snow-covered courtyard, bounded on the far side by a long, low shape that her milkmaid's sense knew at once was a cattle byre. From it, in bursts between the gusts of wild music, came sounds she knew – the earth-rending stamp, the bloodcurdling snort, of a bull prepared for battle.

She crossed to the byre door and listened. The bull must be loose – to and fro, to and fro went its stamping from wall to wall. And, straining her ears, she thought she heard a faint groan.

She pushed open the door and felt the bull's hot breath on her. She saw him standing, black and monstrous in the dim light cast by a lantern, his eyes fixed on her, wicked and red, his battering ram of a head lowered ready to charge.

Then he sniffed, and the rage drowned out of him. He gently licked her hand, and she felt the rasp of his tongue as it curled over her fingers. The queen's black bull calf, Star, had done the same when, before he could eat grass, she had dipped her hands in deep pails of whey gruel and let him lick them dry.

She turned the massive, passive head towards the lantern. Yes, there was the five-pointed white star on his black brow.

"Star! Star!" she whispered and, rubbing his ears, she stepped beside him towards the dark corner, from which came laboured breathing.

A young man stirred painfully as she came near. Passing light hands over him, she found that he was bound hand and foot, too tightly for her to untie him. The eyes in the blood-drained face lifted, looked deep into her own, then closed again.

"It is I, Sappho," she murmured. "Lie still, my prince. Leave everything to me."

She gathered up the weak prince in her strong arms, lifted him, heaved him onto the broad back of the quiet bull.

"Come, Star!" said Sappho.

And out of the byre and the courtyard, through the night and the whirling snow, she led the black bull into the black forest.

It was still snowing and windy when, later that night, a blast on the guest horn at the castle gate summoned the guards. No footprints led to the gate and none led from it; the snow had filled them up as soon as they were made. But there at the guards' feet lay the lost prince, unconscious, bound hand and foot, but, praises be, still alive.

All over the castle, lights were kindled to life, and all over the castle, joy was kindled with them.

Now the queen, watching through the night at her son's bedside, pondered a mystery: "He did not find his own way back alone, bound hand and foot. Someone had brought him. But who? And how?"

Next morning, news came from the royal farm that Star, stolen by Simeon the Sorcerer three years ago, had been found there at dawn, chained in his own byre.

And again the queen thought: "So Star brought the prince home. But who among my son's friends would know how to handle a bull, or even know which had been Star's byre three years ago?"

The days passed, but Prince Pepin still lay in his bed, pale, silent, lost and listless. The queen was old enough to know lovesickness when she saw it.

"Where does she live, this lady you love, my son?" she asked.

"Nowhere, Mother," he answered faintly. "I met her in a dream."

So next day, before the king's daily visit to his son, the queen had the legs of the prince's bed sawn through.

"Why do you do that, Mother?" asked Prince Pepin.

"To get you your heart's desire, my son," she told him. "Lie still. Leave everything to me."

"Someone else said that to me lately," said Prince Pepin quietly, "but I cannot remember who."

When the king came in and sat down with a bump on the edge of the bed, as he always did, *crash* it went, king, prince and all.

"My golden garters! What was that?" asked the king, scrambling to his feet and dusting down his royal robes with his royal handkerchief.

"Our son's heart," said the queen. "It is so heavy that the bed broke under him."

"Heavy with what?" asked the king.

"With love of a lady he met in a dream," said the queen.

"Is that so?" said the king, rolling his eyes. "Get better, my son, and you shall marry somebody real."

But Prince Pepin did not get better.

So, a few days later, again just before the king was due to visit his son, the queen scattered dry crumbs in the prince's bed.

"Why do you do that, Mother?" asked Prince Pepin.

"To get you your heart's desire, my son," she told him. "Lie still. Leave everything to me."

"I remember now," said Prince Pepin dreamily. "It was she who said that before she rescued me."

"Who?" asked the queen.

"She told me her name," said the prince, groping in his misty mind, "but I have forgotten it."

"Now I know a little more," thought the queen. "It was a girl who rescued him."

When the king came in, he sat down with a bump on the edge of the bed, as usual. The prince rolled over to give him room. *Crack, crack, crack* went the dry crumbs under him.

"My golden garters! What was that?" cried the king, frightened out of his wits.

"Our son's heart," the queen told him, "breaking for love of the girl who rescued him."

"Then let him marry her," said the king, "before this heart of his pulls down the whole palace around our ears."

"Whoever she is?" asked the queen.

"Whoever she is," said the king firmly. "And who *is* she?"

"Nobody knows," said the queen. "He has forgotten her name."

"Pah!" said the king. "That is easy. Just make me a list of girls' names, and I shall soon find out."

The queen sat down with a roll of clean parchment, and nibbled the tip of her goose-feather quill.

"Which of my girls would be strong enough to lift him?" she asked herself. "Only my milkmaids. Which of my girls would know about Star? Only my milkmaids."

So she wrote down all her milkmaids' names, and handed the list to the king.

The king put on his gold-rimmed spectacles, and looked over the top of them at the prince each time he read out a name. But the prince lay with his head on his pillow, pale and lost and listless, and did not open his eyes from first to last.

"Your mind does not remember, my son," the queen said. "Let us see if your heart does."

She laid her fingertips on the prince's wrist and asked the king to read the list again.

She could feel her son's pulse, still slow and faint and quiet, as name followed name. Then all at once it gave a mighty leap.

"Stop there, dear," said the queen to the king. And she said to Prince Pepin, "So it was Sappho, my son?"

"Was it?" Prince Pepin answered, still pale and lost and listless.

The queen sent for Sappho. As she came shyly into the prince's chamber, he gave her one look and in two seconds he was out of his bed and across the room and holding her tight in his arms.

When Princess Sappho went with her four-leaved clover to find Simeon the Sorcerer's house again, it had vanished into thin air. And, just as it said in his letter, he has never troubled that kingdom again from that day to this.

And though by now we have forgotten why, to this day we still think it's lucky to find a four-leaved clover.

14. The Shining Loaf

Once there was a king, called King Moneybags, who was sick. Seven royal doctors stood in a row by the king's bedside, and they shook their seven heads at the three black moneybags painted on the shield that the king had had lain over him. Little Princess Cordelia stood with them.

"All the moneybags in the kingdom can't save your honourable father," they told the small princess. "Your best hope is Mother Grana, but she disappeared into the wild lands when cottage loaves went out of fashion."

Cordelia tipped her little gold crown over her left eye to help her to run faster, and away she went – out of the marble bedchamber, down the marble staircase, out at the wrought iron gates, out of the city and over the moor, to the door in the high wall that held the kingdom together. It was locked, and it was padlocked, but it flew open at her touch, and out she shot into the wild lands.

Out of the wild lands loomed a rose-red cottage, with birds singing on its thatch of golden straw. Cordelia went through its open door into a white, bright, spotless, speckless kitchen, with a fire of wheat-straw burning with clear golden flames on the hearth. The homeliest peasant woman Cordelia had ever seen stood at the scrubbed ashwood table, kneading shining bread dough into shining cottage loaves. She was rather like a shining cottage loaf herself.

"Our bread doesn't shine like that," said Cordelia.

"More's the pity," said the peasant woman.

"What makes yours shine?" asked Cordelia.

"The sun in the wheat," said the peasant woman.

"What makes your fire golden?" asked Cordelia.

"The sun in the straw," said the peasant woman.

"Why is that wall around the kingdom?" asked Cordelia.

"To keep people in," said the peasant woman.

"But I got out," said Cordelia.

"Children can," said the peasant woman.

"So did Mother Grana," said Cordelia. "Can you tell me where to find her?"

"You *have* found her," said the peasant woman.

"Quick, Mother Grana!" cried Cordelia then, tugging at her cottage-loaf skirts. "King Moneybags needs you."

They shot out of the cottage and through the wild lands and in at the door in the wall, over the moor and into the city, in at the wrought iron gates, up the marble staircase and into the marble bedchamber.

"Put out your honourable tongue, Your Majesty," said Mother Grana.

King Moneybags put out his honourable tongue.

"Mercy me!" cried Mother Grana. "Your Majesty's honourable tongue is too foul for words. Only one thing can clean it – three crumbs from a shining loaf that is a free gift from your kingdom."

"Who ever heard of a free gift in *my* kingdom?" demanded King Moneybags. "And who ever saw such a thing as a shining loaf?"

"I've seen one," said Cordelia. "In Mother Grana's cottage, out in the wild lands."

"Then I will graciously accept it," said King Moneybags.

"*That* will not clean Your Majesty's honourable tongue," said Mother Grana, "for that would not be a free gift from your own kingdom."

Cordelia tipped her crown over her left eye to help her run faster, and away she went – out of the marble bedchamber, down the marble staircase, out at the wrought iron gates, through the streets of the city, and into a baker's shop.

"Please, Baker, can you bake me a shining loaf?" she asked.

"If you can bring me some shining flour," the baker told her.

Out of the baker's shop she shot, and ran to a mill.

"Please, Miller, can you grind me some shining flour?" she asked.

"If you can bring me some shining grain," the miller told her.

Out of the mill she shot, and ran to a threshing barn.

"Please, Thresher, can you thresh me some shining grain?" she asked.

"If you can bring me a shining sheaf," the thresher told her.

Out of the threshing barn she shot, and ran to a ripe cornfield.

"Please, Reaper, can you reap me a shining sheaf?" she asked.

"If you can sow me some shining seed," the reaper told her.

Out of the field she shot, and ran across the Bridge of the Seasons into a springtime plowed field.

"Please, Sower, can you sow me some shining seed?" she asked.

"If you can fill me a sieve with sunlight in which to soak the seed," the sower told her.

Cordelia held the sieve up and into it streamed the sunlight – and away again out of it.

Then a bird came out of the wild lands, and perched on a branch above her, and began to sing:

> "Sweet, sweet, sweet, sweet!
> My song I give
> As a gift, gift, gift, gift!
> Plaster your sieve
> In each rift, rift, rift, rift!
> Light will not leak away
> If you seal it with clay.
> Fill it! Fill it! Fill it!"

Cordelia filled all the holes with clay, and the sunlight streamed in and filled the sieve to the brim. Then she ran back with it to the sower.

"It was a gift from a bird from the wild lands," she told him, as he stood and gaped in amazement.

"Then let the sowing be a gift, too," said the sower.

He soaked his seed in the sieveful of sunlight, and sowed it; and as he sowed, he thought, "Why do I feel so happy?"

The young corn sprang up and grew green and tall, and ears filled and turned golden, ready for harvest. Cordelia had hardly got her breath back after running before the corn began to shine.

She ran to fetch the reaper, to reap the shining corn.

"It was a gift from the sower and a bird from the wild lands," she told him, as he stood and gaped in amazement.

"Then let the reaping be a gift, too," said the reaper.

And as he reaped a shining sheaf, he thought, "Why do I feel so happy?"

Cordelia ran with the shining sheaf to the threshing barn.

"It was a gift from the reaper, the sower and a bird from the wild lands," she told the thresher, as he stood and gaped in amazement.

"Then let the threshing be a gift, too," said the thresher.

And as he threshed the shining grain and filled a grain bag with it, he thought, "Why do I feel so happy?"

Cordelia ran with the shining grain to the mill.

"It was a gift from the thresher, the reaper, the sower and a bird from the wild lands," she told the miller, as he stood and gaped in amazement.

"Then let the milling be a gift, too," said the miller.

And as he ground the shining flour and filled a flour bag with it, he thought, "Why do I feel so happy?"

Cordelia ran with the shining flour to the baker's shop.

"It was a gift from the miller, the thresher, the reaper, the sower and a bird from the wild lands," she told the baker, as he stood and gaped in amazement.

"Then let the baking be a gift, too," said the baker.

And as he mixed it and kneaded it and shaped it and put it in to bake, he thought, "Why do I feel so happy?"

Cordelia had hardly got her breath back from running when he opened the oven door again and took out the shining loaf.

"Goodness!" he cried. "Just look what shape I have made! This is the first cottage loaf I have made since cottage loaves went out of fashion!"

Cordelia ran with the shining loaf through the streets of the city, in at the wrought iron gates, up the marble staircase and into the marble bedchamber. She thrust the shining loaf into Mother Grana's hands.

"It was a gift from the baker, the miller, the thresher, the reaper, the sower and a bird from the wild lands," she told her.

"Good," said Mother Grana. "That makes it a free gift from the kingdom. Open your honourable mouth, Your Majesty!" ordered Mother Grana. And she dropped in three shining crumbs.

Then King Moneybags put out his honourable tongue.

"As clean as a whistle!" reported Mother Grana.

Outside there sounded a whistle like nothing on earth. Cordelia ran to the window, and she saw that the high wall that ran around the kingdom had disappeared into the wild lands, and the wild lands came pouring in.

The king rose up from his bed. He dressed his honourable self in his golden robes and his golden crown.

"Bring me a scrubbing brush," he told his seven royal doctors, "and a big pot of gold paint."

When they had done so, he borrowed Mother Grana's white starched apron, rolled up his gold cloth sleeves, and tipped his crown over his right eye, to give more power to his elbow. Then he scrubbed the three black moneybags off his shield, and in their place he painted a shining cottage loaf.

15. King Arthur's Gold

Each sunrise Mia led her father's flock of sheep from the fold. They lay busily growing wool all day on a round mound of a hill called King Arthur's Castle, where the grass was dense and lush. (The sheep they had in those days knew a sweet bite of grass when they saw one.)

Each noon Mia sat down by King Arthur's Well. She spread her handkerchief, as clean and white as milk, on the edge of the well, and on her handkerchief she laid a ripe red apple and a crust of good black bread.

"Auntie Frog!" she called.

Auntie Frog popped out of her cold bath in the well (she was a great believer in cold baths), and hopped up to share Mia's meal.

While they ate from the handkerchief, while they drank from the well, Mia told Auntie Frog how on their farm the fences were falling down, the gates were falling off, the walls were falling out, and the roof was falling in, for her father was so poor that he didn't have a flitter to fly with.

"No matter and never mind, child," Auntie Frog

comforted her. "One fine day that farm will be as neat as a new pin."

"Oh, *when*, Auntie Frog?" cried Mia.

"When your sheep turn yellow," said Auntie Frog.

"What could make them do that?" asked Mia.

"Lying on hidden gold," said Auntie Frog.

Mia watched and waited for the curly fleeces to change colour and, believe it or not, one day they did. She ran to the well to tell Auntie Frog. She was so excited that she hardly knew which leg to stand on.

"Didn't I tell you so?" said Auntie Frog, blowing herself up big.

"But where is the hidden gold?" Mia asked. "And why is it suddenly where it wasn't?"

"It is King Arthur's gold," Auntie Frog told her. "From deep in the earth it rises a rooster's stride every year till it lies in his castle. If you can get in before the gold sinks again, a lapful, a crockful and a kettleful will be yours."

"Won't King Arthur mind?" asked Mia.

"Not he," said Auntie Frog. "He knows that those above ground need gold more than those below."

"How can I get in?" asked Mia.

"By the castle door, like an honest person," said Auntie Frog.

"But doesn't King Arthur keep that locked?" asked Mia.

"Of course he does," said Auntie Frog. "Kings do when they settle down to sleep for centuries. But do as you would be done by, and you will find the key."

Mia had taken seven steps – she had taken no more, she

had taken no less – when she heard the woodpecker nestlings squawking to be fed. She saw them popping their heads from their nest hole in the hollow tree trunk in frantic search of lunch and their father. She heard Father Woodpecker himself tapping a distant tree trunk for grubs with his beak of bone. And she saw the slinking stoat, dark and greedy, bear down the defenceless nestlings as his prey.

Flinging her crook at him, Mia heaved up a rock with both hands and with it shut the nestlings into safety. But when the stoat had slunk away, and Mia tried to dislodge the rock, she found it was too firmly wedged in the woodpeckers' doorway.

"No matter and never mind, child," said Father Woodpecker, swooping home with a beakful of delicacies; and with a flourish and flash of green wings, red crest and golden rump, away he flew.

Back he darted with a blue flower in his beak. He flew round the tree trunk nine times against the sun, and then he touched the rock with the flower. The rock fell away and out popped the nestlings all shrill with indignation. Father Woodpecker swooped down to lay the flower in Mia's hand.

Mia ran seven steps – she ran no more, she ran no less – back to King Arthur's Well. Auntie Frog, blowing bubbles, rose out of her bath.

"Didn't I tell you so?" said Auntie Frog, blowing herself up big. "Off with you, child; nine times round King Arthur's Castle with the blue flower in your hand. As soon as you see the door, touch it with the flower, and it will open; wedge it with your crook, and in you must go!"

"And then, Auntie Frog?" gasped Mia, breathing very hard.

"Do not wake King Arthur and his knights," said Auntie Frog. "Tread softly; do not even look at them; do not turn your head or eyes either to left or to right. Let your back face them, let your face turn away from them, as you take your lapful and your crockful and your kettleful of gold. Tiptoe out with the gold, pick up your crook, and there you'll be!"

Mia ran nine times round King Arthur's Castle against the sun, the blue flower in her hand. All at once, there in the side of the grassy mound, she saw a door, framed by great standing stones. When she touched it with the flower, the door swung slowly inward, into a passage bathed in a gentle milky light. Wedging the door open with her crook and holding her breath, her heart in her mouth, Mia stepped across the threshold.

In utter silence she moved along the passage, between walls of rock glittering with quartz and feldspar. In utter silence she passed beneath a lofty gateway into a chamber like a church. Its high roof, studded with rock crystals, was supported on massive alabaster pillars, luminous with their own inner light; from carved arches, soaring and crossing in the dusk above, hung lamps like a giant's pearls.

In the shadows beyond their milky radiance, Mia caught a glimpse of sleeping forms in golden casques and glinting armour. She did not look at them and she did not turn head or eyes either to left or to right. She let her back face them, she let her face turn away from them, as she gathered a lapful, a crockful and a kettleful of gold. For gold lay as thick upon the black and white chessboard floor as fallen leaves lie in an October beechwood.

Knotting up her dress with its lap full of gold, a crock full of gold in one hand, and a kettle full of gold in the other, she tiptoed without a backward glance, as silent as still air, out of that hushed chamber, along the silent passage, over the heavy stone threshold, and there she was!

She picked up her crook, and the door closed silently between the standing stones. When she looked again, the turf lay smooth and green, and she could not even see where door or standing stones had been.

As she went by King Arthur's Well, Auntie Frog popped out of her bath and hopped with marathon leaps to roll her bulging eyes at Mia's glittering treasure.

"Didn't I tell you so?" said Auntie Frog, blowing herself up big. "Drop the blue flower in the well, child, to keep it fresh for other folks who do as they would be done by."

The farm now is spick and span, as bright as a new penny, as neat as a new pin, with a fine fat cow for every day of the year. In fact, there is nothing that is of use on a farm that is not to be found on that one.

"Didn't I tell you so?" said Auntie Frog, blowing herself up big.

THE SEVEN-YEAR-OLD
WONDER BOOK
Isabel Wyatt

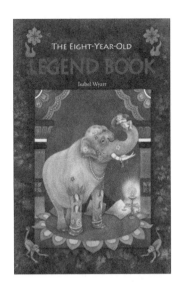

THE EIGHT-YEAR-OLD
LEGEND BOOK
Isabel Wyatt

Isabel Wyatt
LEGENDS OF THE
NORSE KINGS

Legends of
King Arthur
Isabel Wyatt

NORSE HERO TALES

Isabel Wyatt

The King and the Green Angelica
and other stories

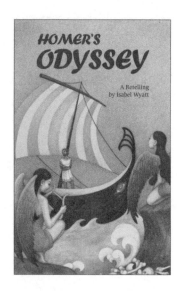

HOMER'S ODYSSEY

A Retelling
by Isabel Wyatt

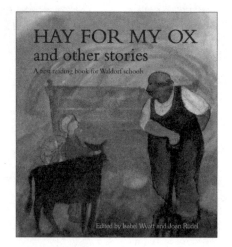

HAY FOR MY OX
and other stories

A first reading book for Waldorf schools

Edited by Isabel Wyatt and Joan Rudel